RETURN TO THE DEEP

MICHAEL BRAY

"The oldest and strongest emotion of mankind is fear, and the oldest and strongest kind of fear is fear of the unknown."
— H.P. Lovecraft, Supernatural Horror in Literature

"There's nothing in the sea this fish would fear. Other fish run from bigger things. That's their instinct. But this fish doesn't run from anything. He doesn't fear."
— Peter Benchley, Jaws

"Call me Ishmael."
— Herman Melville, Moby-Dick

CHAPTER ONE

South Beach, Florida

The heat of the Florida sun had been replaced by campfires, which were spread sporadically down the white sands of the beach. The monotonous song of rolling tide had been joined by the sounds of laughter and the occasional song from an acoustic guitar. Barbecues were fired up, some couples paired off and found intimacy in the shadows. Others were content just to enjoy the ambiance as day gave way to night.

"It's haunted, you know," Fernando said, watching his friend for a reaction.

"Bullshit it is," Jim shot back.

"No, it is," Clayton cut in, dropping the glowing ember of his cigarette onto the beach and crunching it under foot.

"Oh yeah? And how would you know?" Jim asked, taking a swig from his beer and wedging the bottom back into the hollow he'd made in the sand.

"You know my cousin Frankie?"

"Is he the tall one? The one with the buck teeth?" Jim said, biting his lower lip and showing his own less than perfect set.

"Yeah."

"Yeah, I know Frankie, he's a good guy," Jim said, finishing his beer and immediately grabbing another out of the box beside him.

"Yeah," Clayton nodded, flicking his eyes towards Marie, who was watching with interest as she let the surf roll over her ankles. "Well, he told me it all started a few years ago when a guy he knew went swimming out there, and never came back."

"I doubt that," Fernando said, trying to keep casual despite a shiver, which danced down his spine. "We'd have seen it in the news."

"It *was* in the news."

"Oh yeah? Well *I* didn't see it."

"He washed up on the same day of the Boston Marathon explosion. I guess it got lost in the shuffle," Clayton fired back,

1

locking eyes with his friend.

"So what happened to him?" Fernando said, giving a quick glance towards the ocean as it edged its way up the beach.

"They say he drowned, but everyone around here knows what *really* happened."

"What's that?" Marie said, watching the conversation unfold with eyes, which were part curious, part afraid.

Clayton flashed his best smile, the one reserved for girls like Marie who he hoped to add to his ever-growing list of conquests.

"I forgot, you're not from around here, are you?" He said, letting his eyes linger on her bronzed midriff just long enough for her to notice.

"Ignore him; it's just a story, and a stupid one at that," Jim said, watching the tanned, muscular Clayton give the eyes to Marie and feeling a pang of jealousy about his own skinny frame.

"What makes you so sure it's just a story" Clayton fired back, aware that Marie was now watching him with interest. "Everyone around here, locals, I mean, know well enough not to go out there after dark."

"Would somebody just tell me what you're talking about?" Marie said, watching them both now with more than a little frustration.

"Forget it, it's nothing," Jim said, staring out over the ocean as he sipped his beer.

"So why won't anyone tell me?"

"Nothin' to tell," Jim said, spitting in the sand and locking eyes with her, "it's just a dumb story."

"So why won't you just tell it?"

"Hell, I'll tell it," Fernando said, fishing his cigarettes out of his pocket as he sat on the sand and crossed his legs. Without a word, everyone joined him, sitting in a rough circle around the dying embers of their beach fire. They waited for him to light his cigarette, and for a moment, there was only the sound of the tide as it made its endless ebb and flow and surrounded them. Fernando took a deep drag of his cigarette, exhaled, and began to speak.

"Some of you here already know this story or a version of it anyway. This is supposed to be the truth, the real story amid all the bullshit embellishments."

"Check, Jack-a-fuckin'-nory over here," Jim said, chuckling at his own joke. When he saw nobody else was laughing, he cleared his throat and waited for Fernando to continue. He took another lungful of smoke and exhaled, then turned towards Marie.

"Do you remember that thing in the news a few years back about the sea monster sightings around here?"

"Yeah, I remember," Marie said. "Wasn't it supposed to have killed all those people in that boat race?"

"Yeah, the very same."

"The news said it was a shark attack, a rogue great white or something. I remember my dad watching it in the news. I was only around fourteen at the time, so that would have been maybe four years ago I think."

"Five," Fernando said with a grin, "and it was no Great White."

"My dad said the sea monster stuff was a hoax. People just getting carried away with the tale."

"So the papers said, and anyone else who was involved in covering it up at the time." Fernando replied, elongating his grin. "People around here though, know that's not even close to the truth."

"Go on," Marie said, holding his gaze.

Enjoying the attention, Fernando went on. "A buddy of mine called Sam, has a brother who used to work for the government. Low level stuff mostly, but the point is, he overheard stuff. Secret stuff. Do you remember the official story they put out about the boat race attack? Not the shit they put in the news, I'm talking about the official report now."

"I only heard what my dad told me," Marie said, tucking a lock of brown hair behind her ear.

"Well, the official story was similar to the news report. They said it was a school of sharks. Great whites apparently mistook the boats for seals or some shit like that. Everyone knows it was bull, hell, anyone who lives this close to the ocean will tell you that, although whites do occasionally mistake the odd surfer for supper, they sure as hell don't attack in groups. Anyway, that was the official story and like always, the government swept it under the rug until people forgot about it. Funny thing is, the two guys who survived the attack were killed in separate plane crashes within three days of each other, and less than a month after the incident.

For me, that's too much of a coincidence. It seems to me somebody was trying to keep them quiet about what actually happened out there."

"Come on, get on with it," Clayton said, frowning at the attention Marie was giving to his friend.

"Sorry," he said, flashing a grin at them, his brown eyes flickering in the dull glow of the fire. "Anyway, that was the story, and as they had planned, it was all forgotten. So, fast forward a year or so, and my brother's buddy gets discharged from his post with the government. He wouldn't tell anyone why, but my buddy said it was obvious that he was pretty pissed about the situation. One afternoon, Sam comes home to find his brother slumped in the chair, absolutely shitfaced, mumbling on and on about how it was unfair, and it wasn't his fault. Sam was curious, so he started to ask questions. His brother told him how it wasn't sharks, but a whale. A big one. Some kind of undiscovered supersized thing that nobody knew existed."

"That's even harder to believe than the shark story," Marie said.

"I haven't finished yet," Fernando snapped. "As I was saying, he claimed it was some undiscovered kind of whale. He said he was part of a team that traced this thing out to Antarctica of all places, where it was supposed to have made some kind of lair, a cave hollowed out of the ice. They eventually ended up collapsing the cave and crushing this thing inside. Remember that Ross Ice Shelf collapse that happened around the same time these sightings happened?"

"Yeah," Marie said, showing interest again in the story. "That was a pretty big deal too as I remember."

"Well, that was a lie too, or at least the reason it happened was. It wasn't a collapse, but a controlled explosion designed to kill this giant whale and its offspring."

"Offspring?" Marie whispered, flicking her eyes towards the ocean.

"Oh yeah, apparently it had little whale babies with it too. Sam's brother said the mother was killed and one of the babies taken away for study."

"I still don't get it, what does that have to do with here?" Marie said, close to losing interest again.

Fernando jabbed a thumb over his shoulder to the shadow of the hulking aquarium visible down the beach, a black smudge against the twilight. "Rumour is that they took the young one in there for tests, research, all kinds of crap like that."

"Into a public aquarium?" Marie said, shaking her head and dislodging the stubborn bang of hair from behind her ear. "That's the stupidest thing I've ever heard."

"That's the thing," Fernando went on. "It's common knowledge that only a small portion of that place is open to the public. More than half of it is sealed off. You ever noticed how tight the security is in there? There's obviously something in there that nobody wants us to see."

"It all sounds a bit far-fetched," Marie muttered, starting to lose interest and turning her attention back to Clayton.

"No it's true," Clayton said, giving her that grin again. "It's been a bit of a curiosity around here since that thing opened. They say it's closed off, ready to develop future attractions, which, I suppose is plausible, although you have to ask why none of those developments have happened yet."

"Still," Marie said, pointing at Fernando with a half-smile on her face, "how does *he* know so much about it?"

"I just know," Fernando said with a shrug. "The point is, they say the creature's mother wasn't killed in the ice collapse, and tracked its baby to the aquarium. Apparently, it hides in the deep water just off the coast here, feeding on those brave or stupid enough to swim out too far whilst it waits to be returned with its young."

"Oh please," Marie said, chuckling while taking a sip of her beer. "This sounds like a Twilight Zone episode. Surely, you don't believe any of this shit?"

"It's true," Fernando grunted. "People go missing out here all the time. They go out for a swim and never come back. Some people who did make it back to shore say they can hear the spirits of the dead, crying in the darkness, and warning people to stay away from the water."

"Still sounds like an urban legend to me, and a shitty one at that," Marie said.

"Then you swim out there. See if anything gets you," Fernando snapped, put out by her dismissal of his story.

"Screw that," Marie replied, glancing out over the ocean. "I'm not swimming out there just so the rest of you can laugh at me."

"I know how we can find out for sure," Clayton said.

"Fishing rod?" Fernando shot back, hoping his joke would hit the mark. Nobody laughed, and now Marie had turned her intense stare back to Clayton.

"No, not a fishing rod," Clayton said, holding Marie's gaze. "The aquarium."

They all looked at the giant shadow of the domed structure.

"What about it?" Fernando said, surprised how jealous he was becoming of the attention Marie was giving his friend.

"Well, you say it's all true. Marie says not. Why don't we go up there and take a look for ourselves?"

"Hey man," Jim said, shaking his head, "I don't think that's a good idea. If we get caught, I'm gonna be in a world of trouble."

"I'm not suggesting we go break in or anything stupid like that. I'm just saying we could go and take a look for ourselves."

"They have night security up there, I've seen them patrolling the grounds," Jim said.

"I'm game."

Everyone looked at Marie. When she noticed them staring, she flushed and looked at her feet, which were half buried in the sand.

"Alright," Clayton replied with a grin, "what about you?"

Fernando looked at the shadowy structure, then at Marie, and finally at Clayton. There was something in his friend's eyes, some primal competitive edge, and an almost daring look, which gave Fernando little choice. "Okay, let's do it."

"Alright then, let's make a move," Clayton said, getting to his feet and brushing sand from his jeans.

"You wanna do this now?" Jim said, giving Fernando an uncertain glance.

"Why not? The place should be closed now. It should be easy, that is, unless you're all scared of a couple of over the hill security guards."

"No, of course not...alright, I'm in," Jim grunted.

"Let's get to it then."

Clayton started to walk down the beach, Marie in tow and

carrying her sandals. Jim and Fernando hung back, keeping a watchful eye on the looming structure ahead. Jim lit a cigarette and listened to the tide roll against the beach as the group walked towards their destination.

II

The aquarium was an imposing domed structure of glass and steel. During daylight hours, it would be jammed with tourists eager to see the variety of exotic marine life housed within its walls. The outer courtyard, usually as full as the inside with people pausing to grab a snack or a cold drink, or maybe even throw a few coins into the ornate wishing fountain, was completely deserted. Through the array of glass doors fronting the entrance, there was a single light barely penetrating the shadows from the security office.

The group stood across the street, trying a little too hard not to look like they were up to no good.

"So what now?" Jim asked, looking increasingly uncomfortable as he fidgeted from foot to foot.

"Relax," Clayton said, frowning and breaking into a grin, "you're gonna give us away if you don't take it easy."

"Sorry, it's just my old man ain't gonna be too happy if I get busted again."

Clayton nodded. Jim's father was one of the many great American statistics, a narrow-minded bigot who liked guns almost as much as he loved booze and beating the shit out of his family if they ever dared to step out of line. Although none of his friends ever mentioned it, there were slow but sure signs that Jim was following in his father's footsteps. He had already racked up a few petty crimes and a nice collection of arrests in his seventeen years on earth, each of which was seen as another excuse by his drunk of a father to take a belt to him. It was perfectly understandable why Jim wanted to avoid another brush with the law. The last time he had been arrested was after getting drunk and stealing a car belonging to his former high school English teacher, Mr Morrison. Jim had led the police on a hell of a chase, before finally getting himself caught when the tire of Morrison's car screamed enough and blew, slewing the cherry dodge into a fishtail and subsequently a drainage ditch. It was a tale of two halves. The state let him off with a caution and a stern warning that further incidents wouldn't be tolerated. His father unleashed his own brand of justice, and broke three of his son's ribs and bruised his spleen.

Lesson learned.

"It's no good hanging around here out front," Clayton said. "We wanna be around the back. If there's a way in, that's where it will be."

The group started to walk, careful not to rush or to look too interested in their eventual destination. Beyond the entrance to the aquarium, the street became a smattering of gaudy gift shops selling assorted trinkets for the tourists, everything emblazoned with either the word Florida, or a picture of a crocodile. Anything from mugs, to t-shirts to key rings was available. One such store adjoined the perimeter wall beyond the car park of the aquarium, and the group led by Clayton, slipped down the alleyway beside it. To their left, the eight-foot tall wall which surrounded the aquarium complex, and on their right, the grubby white wall of the gift shop.

"This ought to do it," Clayton said, coming to a halt halfway down the natural alleyway. "Fernando, give me a boost."

Fernando scratched at his crew cut, hesitating for a moment before dropping to one knee and cradling his hands together. Clayton stepped into the miniature step and he was boosted up onto the wall, hoisting himself up and sitting one leg on either side.

"Okay, come on," Clayton said, first helping Fernando, then Jim, and finally Marie, up and over the wall.

There were two huge steel loading doors down a steep incline, and rows of dumpsters filled with assorted garbage. Beside the loading ramp was a door marked 'Staff only'.

"That's our way in," Fernando said, sauntering across the deserted yard with an almost nonchalant ease.

"It's locked, you won't be able to get in there without a-"

"One of these?" Fernando said, fishing through his wallet and holding up the key card, stopping Clayton mid-sentence.

"Where the hell did you get that?"

"I have my sources. Come on."

The group huddled by the door as Fernando prepared to use the key. He held the magnetic strip against the reader and paused. "If this doesn't work or sets off any kind of an alarm, be ready to run."

"What does that mean?" Jim said, looking agitated.

Fernando smiled and before there was any further protest, slid the card against the reader. The red light flicked to green and the door clicked open.

"Alright," Clayton said, clapping Fernando on the shoulder. "Nice work."

He pulled the door open and assumed the lead. Fernando held the door open for Jim and Marie, and then followed, closing it gently behind them.

III

The air was much cooler on the other side of the door. Air conditioning units growled high on the walls, and the cavernous space was heavy with shadows.

"I can't see a thing," Jim whispered.

"Hang on," Clayton replied. Seconds later, the room was illuminated by a powerful light emanating from the rear of Clayton's phone.

"Who the hell are you, James Bond?" Jim asked.

"Torch app. Come on, this way." Clayton grunted, leading them towards a set of doors on the left of what looked to be a storage room of some kind.

"How do you know it's that way?" Marie asked. "What about *those* doors?" she pointed to the two other sets of double doors on the opposite side of the room.

Clayton pointed to the pipes, which skirted the top edge of the wall. "Water filtration pipes. They lead that way," he said, nodding towards the doors he was initially heading for. "If they're hiding anything in here the size of this supposed super whale, that's where it will be."

He turned and walked towards the doors, not waiting for anyone to reply. As he knew they would, the others followed.

Clayton tried to open the doors. "Shit. It's locked."

"Come on, man, let's forget this and get the hell out of here," Jim whispered.

Clayton almost felt sorry for him, and could almost see the fear in his eyes in anticipation of his father delivering his own brand of justice if they happened to be caught. "Not yet, we're here now, so we might as well try the other doors."

"I don't like this," Jim countered, shifting his weight from one foot to the other, "it feels…wrong."

"Maybe that's your pussy clenching up on you and telling you to run on home," Clayton said, looking at the others for approval.

"Screw you, man. Don't tell me you don't sense it."

"All I sense is you being scared shitless."

"Maybe he's right," Fernando said. "We could all get in big trouble for this if someone catches us."

"Look," Clayton said, shining his torch beam at them, "if the two of you want to leave, that's up to you. I'm staying. I want to know what's going on here."

"I just think it's a risk, that's all," Fernando countered. "I mean, what does it matter to us anyway? It was just a story. Nobody really knows the truth."

"That's what makes it exciting," Marie whispered. She was staring at Clayton, the look of anticipation and attraction unmistakeable. "I'll go with you, even if they won't."

Fernando felt another pang of jealousy, which in turn, made him think with his groin rather than his head.

"Alright, fine, I'm in too, but just a quick look, then we get out of here," he snapped.

Clayton smiled. "See, that wasn't so hard, was it?" He tipped a wink at Marie as he said it, causing her to break eye contact and look at the floor.

"Fine," Jim muttered, "let's just get on with this."

They crossed the room. The second of the two sets of doors was also locked. The third however, was open. Clayton quietly swung it open and stepped over the threshold.

"Holy shit," he whispered as the others followed.

They were on an enclosed walkway, a corridor of white marble with glass observation windows running the entire length of the corridor. To the right were a series of laboratories, cast in half illumination from the discreet overhead lights. They were pristine, and each glass door to the half dozen labs bore a red painted stamp, which said:

CAUTION!

ABSOLUTELY NO ACCESS TO UNAUTHORISED
PERSONNEL.
ANTI CONTAMINATION MEASURES ARE
IN PLACE AT <u>ALL</u> TIMES

The labs would have been interesting enough on their own, if
not for the view to their right. There, some twenty feet below them,
was an enormous body of water, which looked like a sheet of black
ice in the gloom.

"What the hell?" Clayton said, grinning at Fernando.

"This must be it. This must be what they're hiding," Fernando
replied, breaking into a grin of his own.

"See there?" Clayton said, pointing at the double doors visible
through the window beyond the edge of the lagoon of water. "Those
were the ones that we couldn't get through. You can see where the
pipes run through, and then down the wall and into the water. That's
where we wanted to be."

"What do you think is in there?" Marie said, her breath fogging
the glass as she stared at the water.

"Whatever it is, it's obvious they don't want the public to know
about it."

"What if we-"

Jim was cut off by the shrill sound of the alarm ringing through
the building.

"Shit, run!" Clayton said, turning back and racing back the way
they had come, Jim and Marie not far behind.

"Come on, man, hurry up!" Jim yelled to Fernando.

However, Fernando couldn't move. He thought he had seen a
shadow, something shifting beneath the glassy surface of the water.

"Hey, I think I-" he turned to tell his friends, then for the first
time noticed they were gone, and he was standing alone.

He turned to follow, thanking his luck that he didn't get caught,
when he felt the vice like grip on his shoulder just seconds before he
was tackled to the ground by the security guard.

"Get the hell off me," Fernando grunted as he tried to wriggle
free.

"Fernando?" The guard said, hauling Fernando to his feet.

"What the hell are you doing here?"

"Fuck you, Tom."

Fernando's older brother frowned and released his grip on his sibling's shirt. "How the hell did you get in here?"

Fernando held up the key card.

"You little bastard. That's mine. I had to report it lost last week."

"I only borrowed it."

"Do you know how much trouble you're in?"

The brothers looked at each other, the two of them remarkable in similarity. The same olive complexion, dark eyes, and slightly hooked nose.

"That depends if you let me go."

"My ass will be on the line if I do that. This is breaking and entering, Fred."

Only Tom called him by that name. He hated anyone else to do it, and made a point of letting them know. Tom had always called him that, and it was something neither of them really thought about.

"Come on, you know mom will go postal on me if she finds out about this," Fernando said.

Tom hesitated, looking at his brother and then back over his shoulder.

"Go on; get the hell out of here. You and your friends just stay away from now on, you hear me?"

Fernando nodded. "What will you say to the other guards?"

"There's only old Harry working with me tonight, and he lost interest in the job years ago. Even so, as slow as he is getting up the steps, I wouldn't hang around. Now go home. I'll talk to you later."

"Thanks, bro. I owe you one," Fernando said as he turned to leave.

"Hey, Fred."

Fernando turned around to see his brother's outstretched hand. "Key card."

Fernando handed the card to his brother then turned and jogged after his friends. Tom waited on the walkway staring at the empty door and waiting for Harry to catch up to him. The old man's arrival was preceded by the sounds of his wheezing.

"Whatisit?" he gasped.

"Just kids screwing around."

"You get a look at em?"

"No, they got away."

Harry nodded and took his phone from his pocket.

"What are you doing?" Tom asked.

"You know the rules. Any security breach on here and we have to inform Mr Andrews."

"This wasn't really a breach. Besides, they were just kids. I don't think we need to bother him."

Harry shook his liver spotted head. "Rules is rules, son. Not worth us losin' our jobs over is it?"

"No, suppose not," Tom mumbled, shoving his stolen key card back into his pocket and wondering just what kind of fish was so important that it warranted such intense security. He looked out of the window, staring at the inky surface waters. He thought he saw a flash of movement, and was about to consider looking for a light switch when Harry put a leathery hand on his shoulder.

"Come on, kid, you know the rules. We ain't supposed to have anythin' to do with what's in here."

"Yeah, I know. Aren't you even a little bit curious though, Harry? About what they're doing in here?"

The old man pursed his lips, and ran a hand through his wispy white hair. "Whenever I get curious, I always think about what it did to the damn cat. Now, come on, let's get the hell outta here before we get into trouble ourselves."

Tom nodded and followed the old man, unable to resist another lingering look out of the window to the water below, but whatever he thought he had seen, was gone, and the opaque waters were still again.

CHAPTER TWO

The following morning arrived much like every other day in Florida, the intense heat of the sun already borderline unbearable by eight in the morning. Pristine blue skies devoid of clouds stretched as far as the eye could see, and storeowners all around the aquarium were opening up shop, hoping to entice another fresh glut of tourists into purchasing a souvenir or two as a memento of their holiday.

Tom sat in the staff room, waiting to be interviewed about the break in. He was glad of the time to think ahead of the pending arrival of Andrews. When Harry had made the call, Andrews was on a business trip in Atlanta. Upon hearing of the break in, he had told them to wait for him and he would be there as soon as he could. For as much as Tom knew, it could only lead to bad things, he couldn't help but think about what he thought he had seen in the water, especially since whatever it was seemed important enough to Andrews to drop everything and fly out immediately. His inner voice screamed at him to let it go, and although working as a security guard wasn't exactly a dream career, it was a job, and meant that he could at least pay the bills and afford to eat until something better came along. The door to the office opened and Harry popped his head in.

"Heads up, lad, he's here."

Tom nodded, and waited for Andrews to arrive.

II

Having only ever seen him at a distance, Tom wasn't quite sure what to expect from Andrews. Certainly, he didn't expect to feel quite as intimidated as he sat opposite the man, who was staring at him intently. Tom thought he had one of those faces- the kind that belongs to people who have seen and done things reserved for a certain small percentage of the population. His dark hair was parted at the side, and although it was greying at the sides, he wore it well, and it gave him an almost regal look. He had a neatly trimmed beard, which like his hair, was starting to lose its natural colouration. Most impressive however, were his eyes, which shimmered as if diamonds set in rough leather. The idea of being able to convince Andrews that he knew nothing about the people who broke into the facility seemed just a little bit more difficult.

"So," Andrews said with a sigh, "let's go over this one more time. The silent alarm on the rear staff door was triggered at nine forty six, and yet, neither you nor Mr Benjamin responded until ten-oh-five when the interior motion sensor was triggered, correct?"

"Yes sir."

"So, forgive my lack of understanding, but why such a gap? Shouldn't your response have been immediate?"

"Yes sir."

"So, would you care to explain to me why it wasn't?"

Tom paused, still unsure what to do. The reason neither he nor Harry had seen the silent alarm is because they weren't paying attention. Harry was sleeping in his chair, feet up on the desk. Tom had been on his laptop chatting to his girlfriend. Of course, if he told Andrews that, they would both be fired, and so the two of them had concocted a cover story.

"Well, sir, the truth is, it was an unfortunate coincidence. Harry - uh, Mr Benjamin had gone to use the bathroom. I offered to make coffee."

"So you're telling me your post was unmanned?"

"Only for a few minutes, sir. We came back and noticed the alarm and responded immediately."

"And these intruders, you say they were children?"

"Teenagers."

Andrews nodded, and folded his hands on the desk. "How old are you?"

"Twenty six, sir."

"You work out?"

"Yes," Tom said, caught off guard by the strangeness of the question.

"Thought so, you look fit and healthy."

Tom said nothing, not sure where Andrews was going.

"So, I ask myself how these teens managed to so easily evade you and escape without you being able to apprehend even one of them."

"I'm sorry, sir, I take full responsibility," Tom said.

Andrews stared at him for a few seconds, then turned his icy stare away from Tom and grinned. "Well, no harm done in the end. Mistakes happen, that much is a given. One thing I will say to you Mr..."

"Young," Tom said.

"Mr Young, is that although I will tolerate a mistake once, I don't expect it to be repeated."

Tom nodded, unsure what was happening.

"With that in mind," Andrews went on, "I want you to personally oversee an upgrade to our security systems. I want you to ensure that this incident isn't repeated."

"Sir, I don't have the authority..."

"You do now. I'm giving it to you. If anyone tries to question you or stop you, tell them to speak to me."

"I don't understand, sir, I'm just a security guard. Why me?"

"Because you've had your one chance. I'm confident you will do whatever it takes to makes sure my instructions are followed to the letter, otherwise, it will cost you your job. Understood?"

"Yes, I understand."

"Also understand this is not a promotion. Although this will certainly mean much more work and responsibility, you will remain at your current pay grade."

"I understand, sir," Tom said.

"Good. I hope I don't have to speak to you in this way again, Mr Young. I need to know my staff can be left to do the job they are paid to do. Are we clear?"

"Yes sir."

"Very good," Andrews said, standing and removing his glasses, slipping them into the breast pocket of his jacket. "Now, if you will excuse me, I'm late for an appointment."

Tom could only watch as the enigma known as Andrews swept out of the room in a cloud of expensive aftershave, leaving the minimum wage security guard confused as to what exactly was expected of him.

Outside, Andrews was met by his head scientist, a brilliant but socially frigid man named Neil Barker. Barker fidgeted as Andrews strode past him, almost having to jog to keep up.

"This is completely unacceptable," Barker said as they strode through the vast array of fish tanks open to the public.

"Relax, Neil, I'll deal with it."

"It might have just been kids, but what if it's someone else next time? What if the press get in?" he hissed. "I've been requesting a security upgrade for this facility for over two years now. Surely, now you will agree to my request?"

"Look, I'm arranging for security to be beefed up internally. As well as that, I'll speak to Tomlinson and see if we can get a skeleton crew down here to ensure our restricted areas remain that way."

They strode past the knee level open enclosure containing several dark skinned terrapins and down through one of the many doors labelled staff only.

"You really think Tomlinson will authorise a team to come out here?" Barker said. "He's already pissed at how much money this is costing the government. Do you know what he called it? He said it was a-"

"A financial black hole, I know," Andrews said, interrupting the scientist.

They arrived at another door, this one without a handle. To the right was a keypad. Andrews punched in his five digit code and he was granted access, the door opening with a pneumatic hiss. Beyond were more laboratories, stark white rooms filled with scientists hard at work.

"Look, Martin, I'm not against you here, it's just... I worry about the future of the project," Barker said, nervously twisting his wedding ring around his finger.

"I worry too. The fact is, Tomlinson is right. This *is* a financial black hole. We have spent hundreds of millions of dollars over the last five years and without a shred of progress to show for it. To be honest, I'm surprised we've lasted this long."

"We're trying, Martin. This isn't just a simple case of cloning a sheep. This is a unique species, a one of a kind, which is new in every way. We're breaking new ground as we go, learning every day. Plus, I don't need to remind you the sheer size of the subject makes taking fresh blood and tissue samples incredibly difficult."

Andrews stopped and smiled at the scientist, the expression without humour. "Size?" He said as the smile faded. "How big is our girl these days?"

"A little over eighty two feet."

"Eighty two," Andrews said with a smile. "You know, her mother was quite the spectacle. Well over three hundred feet. Closer to four, now I think about it."

"This one would be the same if it got out into the open. It's only size limited by its environment."

"I know. What I want to hear from you, Neil, is that there is some progress with the cloning."

"We're making steady steps," the scientist mumbled.

"Tomlinson will want something more concrete than that."

"Jesus, Martin, give me a break. I'm working my ass off here, we all are. I need more time."

"Don't shoot the messenger. I'm on your side," Andrews said. "In a way, it's a good thing the government has invested so much money in this already."

"Why?"

"Because it means they'll be reluctant to pull the plug with no return for their investment. That said, they would only do that for a certain length of time. We really need results and fast."

"I don't know what you want from me, Martin. It's not as if we haven't been trying. It's all hands on deck as it is. You saw the results of those early clone attempts. Is that what you want to present to Tomlinson?"

"No, of course not."

"Then please, let me work. As soon as I have something, I'll be in touch."

"I know you will. I don't mean to press you on this, but if you only knew the sacrifices it took to get that creature here..." Andrews trailed off, his mind drifting back to a time he had tried so hard to forget. "Anyway," he said, blinking away the memories, "I have to go. I'll try to buy you some more time."

"That's all it's a case of. They have to understand the uniqueness of the situation. I'm doing everything I can to perfect this. You have my word."

"I know that, believe me, I hate having to be the bastard who delivers the news. Chain of command and all that shit," Andrews said with a shrug.

"You don't have to apologise, just keep Tomlinson and his people off my back and let me and my team do our job."

"Alright, leave it with me. I'll do what I can."

The two men shook hands and went their separate ways. Barker went straight to his office and closed the door. He sat at his desk and sighed, then took the bottle of scotch out of his desk drawer along with the glass he kept in there. He poured himself a single, then changed his mind and made it a double, taking a sip as he picked the throwaway mobile phone out of the back of the drawer and switched it on. He took another drink as he waited for the handset to power up, then dialled the only number, which was stored into it.

"It's me," he said as the line connected, "we need to meet up. I can't delay this any longer."

He took another sip of his drink as he listened.

"No, I can't. It has to be now."

He listened again, trying to convince himself the guilt would go away, especially when he got the money. That would make everything much easier.

"Alright," he said as he grabbed a pen from his desk and opened his notepad, "where do you want me to meet you?"

CHAPTER THREE

The harsh lights of TV studios had gone from something to be nervous and tense about, to a home away from home for Clara Thompson. Certainly, of everyone who was involved with the initial hunt for the giant creature, which had changed all of their lives, she had changed the most. The once quiet marine biologist had become something of a celebrity, and slowly but surely, had grown accustomed to the unrealistic lifestyle enjoyed by the rich and famous. She remembered her first television interview, the way she had stared bug eyed at the camera in clothes, which she felt, didn't reflect the person she really was. Now, those same clothes fit well, and the glare of the lights was tolerated because she knew it would make her look good on screen. She had cut her hair short, and even though she was wearing too much makeup, still looked stunning as the camera pulled her into focus.

"Welcome back to Breakfast with America. I'm Dawn Hinchcliffe, and with me today, I have a very special guest. She's the author of the bestselling novel, 'Terror Beneath the Waves', and everyone's favourite celebrity face, Clara Thompson. Clara, welcome to the show."

"Thank you," Clara said with a smile. Remembering to be polite, and remembering that the camera was her friend.

"Now, let me get right to the point. Many people who have read the book have said that it's so realistic in its execution, they have wondered if it is actually based on fact rather than fiction. Can you tell us now, definitively, what your inspiration was for this book and how you managed to make it so visceral and believable?"

She smiled, a well-practiced expression for the benefit of the media. "Dawn, I've heard these insane theories about the story being based on fact. I can categorically assure you this is entirely a fictional story. I mean, have you read it? I'm sure if it was based on truth, the world would know there was a giant sea monster out there."

"Still, many people, me included, have seen alleged leaked documents stating that you were involved in a secret government project five years ago, which is said to be the basis of this book."

The Media virgin, Clara, would have been thrown off by such a question, maybe even stuttered her way through a half-baked answer. This Clara, though, was a veteran, and went on without missing a beat.

"I think the key word there is alleged, Dawn. Everyone knows the internet is a cesspool of misinformation. I have to admit that reading some of the insane theories about my book was a whole lot of fun."

"Those alleged documents which claim this is a factual situation also state that you were subject to a gagging order of some kind preventing you from telling the story of what happened, and that this novel is a thinly veiled way to get around that and tell the story of what really happened."

Clara smiled again, making a conscious effort to remain calm. "To what end? If these allegations were true, why would I risk telling such a story knowing what the consequences would be? It makes no sense."

Like a shark smelling blood, the veteran presenter moved in for the kill. "Actually, some say it makes perfect sense. The book talks of locations and procedures which are known not only to be actual locations for the alleged sea monster sightings off the California coast, but also details military procedures, which some say only a person with inside knowledge would know. What is your response to that?"

"It's called research, Dawn, and it's my job as an author to make the plot as believable as possible. Nothing more."

"I would like to read an excerpt to our readers, a section of the book from around two thirds of the way through," Dawn said, opening the book to the marked page. "They followed it, deep into Antarctic waters. For every degree the temperature dropped, their fear increased, all of them except Cassidy, the rookie fisherman who had undertaken this trip with a thirst for vengeance against the beast, which had slain his family. For the rest of the crew, it was a journey into the unknown. For Cassidy, it was a chance to come face to face with the beast and finally avenge the death of those he held close."

She closed the book and set it aside. "I want to ask you about the character of Cassidy."

"Go on," Clara said, sensing things were starting to turn for the worse.

"His actions and description within the book closely resemble the life of Henry Rainwater, a local fisherman who was also linked, along with you, in those very same documents which were leaked online."

"I don't hear a question there," Clara snapped.

"Well, my question, Miss Thompson, is can you confirm to our viewers that the character of Cassidy is based on the real life Henry Rainwater? The man who you were known to be involved with on a romantic level in the months following the alleged secret military operation is said to be the basis for your novel."

"I came here to talk about the book. Not my personal life."

"This *is* about the book. Cassidy is a character you claim to have created, a character who shares coincidental similarities with a man who you were involved with, and also linked to the supposed secret project. I think it's a fair question and one which our viewers would be interested in hearing the answer to."

"It's true. I dated Rainwater for a while, although it had nothing whatsoever to do with anything related to my work. Whatever he did or didn't do relating to these documents you keep talking about, I don't know. You'll have to ask him. All I know about Henry Rainwater is that he's a worthless drunk and my time with him was a mistake I would prefer to forget."

"Even so, can you tell us if Cassidy is based on him?"

"If it is, it's unintentional, perhaps some subconscious act during the creation of the manuscript. My book is a work of fiction. Any similarity to people in the real world is entirely coincidental. It says so right there on the copyright page." She managed a smile, barely as the assault continued.

"But our viewers would like to know-"

"No. If you want to talk about the book, that's fine. It's why I agreed to do the show. If you continue to discuss things irrelevant to it, then I'll gladly terminate the interview and leave right now."

She glanced to her agent, a wiry bird like woman with skin like rhino hide, who was squirming off camera at the way the interview was panning out.

"Okay, back on track then," Dawn said, completely unmoved by Clara's outburst. "The book was finished almost two and a half years ago and is only now being released. Why the delay?"

"Well, Dawn, there are marketing strategies, editing decision's to be made, cover artwork to be decided on. It's a long process."

"What do you say to the allegations that the reason for the delay was due to several government court orders trying to stop the book from being released?"

"That's absolute rubbish, and frankly, it reeks of lazy journalism."

Dawn reached to the table beside her and handed over several documents. "Those are copies of the court orders in question."

"Where did you get these?" Clara said, leafing through the photocopies.

"My question to you, is why would the government try to stop the release of this book if there wasn't some truth to the claims surrounding it?"

"Okay, look, I warned you," Clara said, standing and unclipping the microphone from the front of her blouse. "This interview was supposed to be to promote my book, not for you to attack me."

Without a pause, the presenter went on. "This is your opportunity to answer these allegations. This isn't a-"

Clara was already walking away, striding off the set and past the cameras towards the exit.

"What the hell was that, Mary?" She said as she strode past her agent, who hurried to keep up.

"I'm sorry, I had no idea."

"It was a damn witch hunt. They hung me out to dry."

"Look, don't worry about it," the agent said as they walked towards the exit, "I'll deal with this."

"I don't want this to air. It will damage my reputation."

"Remember, all publicity is good publicity."

"They made me look like a fool!" Clara hissed.

"No, what they did was make people curious. Curious enough to buy the book."

"At what cost?"

"Look, Clara, you have nothing to worry about. Sales are still strong. We're number two in the best sellers list. Another couple of weeks of promo, and we could hit the top spot."

She would normally be ecstatic at such news, and yet, she was so angry following the grilling she had just received, she couldn't let it sink in.

"Also," Mary said as they exited the studio into the car park, "I have news for you that might make you happy."

"Go on."

"I managed to get the publishers to agree to buy a sequel. The first book was so good, they want more."

"I'm not so sure I'm ready for that," she said.

"Are you kidding me?" Mary replied, coming to a halt at Clara's cherry red Porsche. "The first book was one of the most creatively strong pieces I've ever read in twenty plus years in the business. You have a gift. The way I see it, if you want to prove people wrong and silence them about this based on reality crap, then a strong sequel is the way to do it."

"I'm not sure."

"Come on, I know you can do it. My job is to do what's best for you. This is one of those times when you should listen to me."

As horrified and unprepared as she felt, she knew refusing to do it would only raise more questions about the origin of the first story.

"Alright, I'll do it."

"Good girl," Mary said. "This will go towards silencing some of these people causing trouble."

"Thanks, Mary."

"Anytime. Hey, between you and me, is any of it true? Not that it matters to me, I'm just curious."

"Of course not," Clara snapped, "it's all bull."

"That's good enough for me. I'll see what I can do about censoring this interview. In the meantime, you start thinking about a follow up story. You can do this, I know it."

The two women hugged, and Clara got into her car, watching her agent leave. With nobody looking at her, she could finally drop the act, and slumped into her seat and started to cry.

CHAPTER FOUR

Tomlinson's office was located in the innermost ring of the Pentagon. Andrews sat on the opposite side of the polished oak desk and waited for the grilling to stop. Tomlinson slammed his fist on the tabletop.

"I don't want to hear *soon*, I need results now," the white haired commander raged.

"Sir, please. I've spoken to the team and relayed just how urgent this is. They have doubled their efforts."

"Do you know how much Project Blue has cost since we gave you the reins?"

"No sir, I'm not privy to the exact amount."

"Six hundred and eighty million dollars, that's how much."

"All I can do is apologise and assure you we're working as hard as we can, sir," Andrews said.

"When you took over from Russo, you assured me you would have results within a year," Tomlinson snapped.

"With all due respect, sir, you know the kind of complications we encountered. This is a brand new species. The cloning-"

"I don't want to hear excuses," Tomlinson said, raising a hand, "I want results."

"We all want results," Andrews countered. "You know well enough what I've had to sacrifice in life for this. I lost my wife, my family, and all for this damn monster."

"It's your job. You get paid well for it."

"What happened back in Antarctica was more than any man should have to endure. Job or no job, you weren't there. It's impossible for you to understand, *sir*."

Tomlinson leaned back in his plush leather chair, letting the silence linger for a few seconds. "Look, Martin, don't think I don't appreciate what you did, or what you had to endure. That business with Russo was an unfortunate case of misjudgement-"

"Misjudgement? You put a damn psychopath in charge of the

mission. He was reckless and dangerous. I thought the government would have appreciated the project having a little stability under my command."

"It's not the stability, it's the cost. Like it or not, money talks and I'm the one who has to justify why we're spending so much without anything to show for it."

"The cloning is progressing well, if you check the most recent reports-"

"Oh, I checked," Tomlinson said, opening his desk drawer and removing a brown envelope, which he opened, removing the papers from inside. "I see here after a year of still births, the only two living specimens you were able to produce were deformed beyond any recognition. Hardly a suitable return for our investment," he said, tossing the papers back on the desk.

"Sir, you have to understand. This is a unique species, a one of a kind. It will take time to-"

"No martin, you need to understand. Project Blue was meant to be the next step in marine biological warfare. Since the Korean War and the tensions with Russia, the country is on edge. Hell, the *world* is on edge."

"All due respect, sir, the Korean war was four years ago. Even if everything with Project Blue had gone to plan, we wouldn't have been placed to interfere."

"Oh, I know that. The north was always going to attack the south. It was just a question of when. What caught us with our pants down was the fact they had nuclear capabilities and we didn't know. The president is keen to make sure we bulk up our defences, especially as far as the Russians go."

"I don't know what you want me to say, sir."

"I don't want words. I want results. Now, tell me about this break in at the facility."

"It was nothing really, just kids screwing around. I'm dealing with it."

"I don't like the fact that kids managed to so easily enter a government facility seemingly at will."

"It was an oversight. Security is being increased. It won't happen again."

Tomlinson didn't offer a response. Instead, he observed

Andrews, who could only sit there and endure the stare of his superior. "As it happens," he said eventually, "we have procedures in place for just such a breach of security."

"It wasn't a breach as such, sir -"

"Let me finish," Tomlinson snapped.

Andrews did as instructed, and listened as Tomlinson continued.

"As I was saying, we have procedures in place for such a breach as this. Because of the public nature of the facility, it was only ever intended as a short term holding location. What I want you to do is prep the creature for relocation."

"Sir," Andrews said just a little too quickly, "moving this creature would be incredibly dangerous."

"As is the chance of the public discovering its existence. It only takes one lapse, Andrews, a lapse that has already happened. As I was saying, I want the creature ready to move within the week."

"To where, sir? The Florida location has everything we need to manage the project. Moving the creature will set us back even further."

"I want the creature transported to Tampa. There it will be loaded onto a transport ship which will deliver it to the Titus."

"Sir, the Titus was only intended to hold the creature for short periods. It needs more space to be able to swim-"

"Dammit, Andrews! This isn't a family pet we're talking about. This is a military owned product. One that we have decided needs to be transported to a new location. You and your team will continue your work on board the Titus. The laboratories are more than adequate for your needs."

"Sir, please. This creature is unique. The risks involved in trying to transport it are huge. What will we say to the public when they see this thing on the back of a flatbed truck being driven in plain sight of everyone?"

"You don't think we have a contingency plan for just this kind of a situation?"

"Sir, I won't saying that. I'm simply pointing out that the risk as far as I can see outweigh the rewards."

"You need to look past your personal involvement in this project," Tomlinson said. "We have designed a special transportation vehicle to move it. Twenty eight wheels and a rear bed plenty big enough to transport the creature. It will be covered with tarps and temperature controlled moisture blankets for the duration of the journey, in addition to which, it will be heavily tranquilised. It will be quite safe."

Andrews could barely hide his anger and frustration. It was only the respect he had for Tomlinson, which allowed him to hold his tongue. Even so, every instinct within him said this was a bad idea, and as much as he would like to be able to change Tomlinson's mind, he knew exactly how stubborn a man he was.

"Yes sir," he said with a sigh of resignation, "I'll make the arrangements."

"Good. The transport will arrive at the Florida facility within the week. Be ready."

"Yes sir. I'll handle it."

"Good," Tomlinson said, for the first time seeming satisfied. "This is your last chance, Andrews. If we don't see results, then we're prepared to cut our losses on this. If you and your people want to keep your jobs, this is the time to give us something concrete."

"Yes sir," Andrews said, now only wanting out of Tomlinson's office as soon as possible.

"This isn't personal, Andrews," Tomlinson said, folding his hands on the desk. "This is just chain of command. My superiors give me shit, so I pass it on to you. It's how this works. If it were up to me, we should have left this creature to die in the ice with its mother."

Andrews said nothing, hoping his silence would lead to him being allowed to leave.

"Well, that's all I need from you right now," Tomlinson said.

Andrews stood and walked to the door. There was so much he wanted to say, so many reasons he wanted to present to Tomlinson as to why the plan to move the creature was a bad one, and yet, knew that his words would go unheard. Instead, he exited the office without looking back.

II

Clayton, Jim, and Marie sat on the beach, basking in another picture postcard Florida summer day. Cloudless blue skies, white sand beaches, and gentle rolling seas were the lure for many of the tourists who had come out to top up tans or socialise with friends. For the group of three friends however, their reasons were different. Even though none of them would say it, they took turns in glancing towards the dome of the Ocean World facility, its glass and steel facade glittering in the sunlight.

"Here he comes," Clayton said, blowing cigarette smoke out of his nostrils and pushing his bare feet deeper into the soft sand.

The others turned to watch as Fernando walked towards them, his eyes hidden by dark sunglasses, camera hanging by the strap around his neck and swinging against his body as he navigated the crowds. He sat with his friends, a light sweat on his brow.

"Here, you look like you could use this," Jim said, handing over a bottle of water from the ice box.

"Thanks," Fernando replied, unscrewing the cap and taking a drink.

"So, what's the story?" Clayton asked.

"Definitely something going on up there. There were two deliveries, one at the standard loading entrance. It looked to be food for the fish in the public area of the facility." He powered on the digital camera and navigated through the photographs he had taken, showing the group.

"After that, another delivery arrived at the back door where we snuck in. This one was a lot bigger."

He scrolled through the pictures of staff unloading huge packages from the truck with a forklift truck.

"Is that-" Marie said.

"Yeah, it's meat," Fernando cut in. "Frozen slabs of meat."

"Why the hell would they deliver meat to an aquarium?" Clayton said, leaning in to get a closer look at the photos.

"Exactly," Fernando said, "and look at the quantity. That ruck is full of the stuff."

"That aquarium tank was big," Marie said. "It shouldn't be a surprise to see them getting enough food to keep whatever is in there healthy."

"I don't know of any whales that eat raw frozen meat like that," Clayton replied with a grin. "Sharks maybe, but not whales."

"You ever hear of the Megalodon?" Jim said.

"No, what's that?" Clayton asked.

"It was a cousin of the great white shark. My dad has a book about them. They were huge, over eighty feet long. Supposedly, they went extinct along with the dinosaurs, but people still say they could exist."

"Well, whatever they have in there, they're keeping it under lock and key," Fernando said. "There's a ton more security in place now, too."

"So what do we do?" Marie asked.

"There isn't much we can do," Clayton said, seeming to lose interest a little. "There's no way we'll get back in there now."

"Not necessarily," Fernando said.

They looked at him and waited for him to elaborate. "The key card I used to get us in there the other day belongs to my brother. He works security."

"I can't see him risking his job to help us though," Jim said.

"No, I wasn't strictly thinking about him. His girl works there too. Gift shop. She's into all this animal rights stuff. If we show her these pictures, maybe she'll help us."

"It's risky," Clayton said, "what if she blabs to your brother?"

"It's not like we'll be any worse off for it. At least this way, we might have a chance to find out what's going on in there."

"You think she'll go for it?" Jim asked.

"I think there's a chance. I can ask her anyways. Won't do us any harm."

"Let's say she snoops around and finds something," Clayton said, as he lit up yet another cigarette, "then what?"

"It all depends what she finds. It's obvious enough that something's going on in there. I just want to know what it is," Fernando replied, looking at the group in turn.

"Alright, count me in again," Clayton said.

"Me too," Marie added.

"Yeah, why not? We've already come this far," Jim said, looking less certain than his friends.

"Alright," Clayton said with a grin, "that's settled then. How soon can you talk to your brother's girl?"

"Tonight," Fernando said, shutting off his camera. "I'll show her the photos; see if she'll snoop around for us. Chances are, she's heard some of the rumblings of what's going on in there. With any luck, she'll be willing to help."

CHAPTER FIVE

Ocean World had been closed to the public for more than two hours. The staff of more than fifty animal feeders and carers had gone home, as had the team of scientists in the area of the building sealed off from the public. Andrews walked around the perimeter edge of the two thousand square foot lagoon, the water on its surface a shimmering, undulating blanket. He looked out at the body of water, and as still as it was, could almost sense the giant which lurked somewhere in its depths.

At one end of the lagoon was a winch loaded with a harness, inside of which was the half ton slab of beef. Pressed to shape and frozen to specification for the specific use of the aquarium, it was the best and safest way to feed the creature. The frozen block of meat glistened under the dull lighting and was already starting to defrost.

Usually, there was a specific team charged with feeding the creature once every three days. In the wild, its need to feed would be much greater, however, in the confines of the aquarium and without the need to hunt, a three-day feeding cycle was deemed sufficient to maintain the health of the creature. Andrews had let the usual feed team go home, and as was his way on occasion, had decided to operate the winch himself. He walked to it, footsteps echoing through the cavernous chamber. He went through his mental checklist, finally, ensuring the chains were securely attached to the meat. Despite being made of two-inch thick stainless steel links, they were still pocked and scratched from countless encounters with the creature's fourteen inch teeth. As strong as the chains were, it wasn't unusual for them to be destroyed during the feeding frenzy, and swallowed by the creature with its meal. To combat this, the chain was routinely changed every third week. Andrews made a mental note to remind his staff to replace the current chain, then remembered he wouldn't have to, as this was likely to be the last time the creature would feed from it before it was transported to Tomlinson's waiting battleship.

He paused for a moment, enjoying the eerie silence of the cavernous space, then started up the winch, which growled to life and shattered the quiet. The wake came almost immediately, a body of displaced water rolling slowly from the far side of the water, drawn in by the familiar vibrations of the crane through the concrete, which signalled feeding time had arrived. No matter how many times he saw it, Andrews always drew breath, always gasped. It took an extraordinary effort not to step back away from the edge as the slow moving wake rolled closer.

With a nervous smile, Andrews activated the winch controls, lifting the slab of meat into the air and swinging it further out over the edge of the lagoon. Bloody melt water dripped into the lagoon, each drop sensed by the creature that circled below the meat, the water churning as it was displaced. Andrews hesitated, waiting for the right time to give the creature its meal.

He pressed the green 'release' button, the chain unrolling as the meat plunged towards the water. No sooner had the slab of beef impacted than the lagoon exploded in a green grey surge of energy. Andrews stared, breath held as the creature savaged the beef, shaking its head and sending bloody chunks drifting towards the bottom of the lagoon. The chain groaned in protest as the creature rolled on top of the meat, wrapping its tentacles around the harness as it tried to pull it deeper. Andrews couldn't believe the sheer power of the animal, and could see why Tomlinson was so intent on harnessing such a force of nature for the defence of the country. The initial idea of trying to capture the creature's mother seemed like utter madness, and it would have been a disaster. The thrashing and churning in the water subsided, leaving the lagoon once again still and calm, the only evidence of any disturbance being the tiny chunks of bloody flesh, which bobbed on the surface. For the first time, Andrews wondered if perhaps Tomlinson was right, and the best outcome for everyone would have been if the creature had suffered the same fate as its parent. No matter how he tried to convince himself otherwise, there was no place in the modern world for such a beast.

II

Joanne Penn had just celebrated her twenty third birthday. The daughter of a prominent Miami judge, it had always been expected that she would follow her father into the world of law. However, she discovered from a very early age that such things didn't interest her, and thought there was too much to see and do in the world without spending countless hours in dusty courtrooms, judging other people and hearing details of how cruel and horrific humanity could be. Instead, she had made the conscious decision to make the most of life, and experience as many different things as she could. Although attractive, Joanne was what would be considered as plain amid the bronzed, cosmetically enhanced bodies, which sauntered around the Florida beaches. Slim with tanned skin smattered with freckles and green eyes, which complemented her dark brown hair, she still managed to avoid much of the attention from the opposite sex, mostly because unlike many girls her age, she wasn't an extrovert. She didn't drink, she didn't have any tattoos, and she hadn't rebelled as a teen. She had drifted along under the radar, making her grades in school and college, and then taking the job at Ocean World. She took it not because she had to, but because she thought it would be a fun place to work, surrounded by children, families, and of course, the plethora of sea creatures.

Her relationship with Tom had happened quite by accident. She had noticed him on his regular patrols of the building, and couldn't deny the physical attraction to him. He was tall and muscular, with strong facial features and piercing eyes. Even so, those early months had been nothing more than a distant relationship between work colleagues, a nod in the hall, a lingering glance in passing. It was only when someone tried to steal something from the gift store and security was called that she had a chance really to speak to him, and discovered to her delight that the two were a seemingly perfect match. They shared a similar philosophy in life, one that was in favour of doing what made you happy rather than what society expected of you. They also shared the same interests and opinions in music, politics, and animal rights. They were perfect for each other and from that first meeting, had spent almost every day together in some way. Almost a year into their relationship, she couldn't be happier.

It was because of her unconditional love for Tom that she had agreed to help Fernando. She had often wondered what was in the sealed off section of the aquarium, and it was one of the few things Tom wouldn't talk to her about. Fernando had shown her the photos they had taken outside the building, and told her of their suspicion that there was something being held there, which was for some reason kept secret. She had always had a soft spot for animals, especially doing everything she could to fight against cruelty. She had been instrumental in helping with the campaigns in 2014 and 15 designed to force SeaWorld to stop keeping orcas in captivity, rejoicing when the motion was finally passed in early 2016. As much as she liked her job, she absolutely would not tolerate animal abuse, and so, it hadn't taken much convincing at least to see if she could find anything out.

Remaining as calm as possible, she had managed to slip within the restricted area and see what was happening. She walked down an interior corridor, a place she had never seen before in the almost two years she had worked there. She knew she shouldn't be there, and that if someone should challenge her as to what she was doing in the pristine white corridor, she would have no answer. Still she went on, curiosity guiding her and doing a fine job of silencing her rationale. Off the corridor were two further doors. One of them was labelled with a sign that read:

Pump maintenance access.
Strictly NO unauthorised personnel.

For someone as curious as she was, such a warning was only going to be met with one reaction. She quietly opened the door and slipped inside. An iron staircase led down to a curved corridor that was lined with pipes. The corridor was dark, lit only by subtle low wattage strips set at intervals in the floor. Ahead, she could see another door, the sign this time even more intriguing.

OBSERVATION AREA
!!!WARNING!!!
NO MOVEMENT IN PRESENCE OF SUBJECT!
NO CAMERAS / MOBILE PHONES!
NO ARTIFICIAL LIGHT SOURCES!

NO ADMITTANCE WITHOUT PRIOR AUTHORISATION!

She inched closer to the door, comforted by the pneumatic hum of the pipes on the walls, which was the only thing other than her own ragged breaths that punctuated the silence. She took out her phone and snapped a shot of the door and another of the warning sign, noting that here in the bowels of the building that she had no reception of any kind. Slipping her phone back into her bag, she inched towards the door.

There appeared to be no locking mechanism that she could see. The steel door was set back in its frame a good three inches, but appeared to be unremarkable despite the stringent warnings on its front. As was her way, she didn't dwell or ponder, but acted on her first instinct, pulling open the door and stepping over the threshold.

It took a few seconds for her eyes to adjust to the gloom. In here, there was no artificial lighting of any kind. The only reason she could see was due to the undulating blue waves and ripples that were thrown on the wall from the twenty five foot long, six foot high viewing window, which looked out into a murky blue-green underwater landscape. She realised she was holding her breath, and let it out in a long slow exhale. Beside the window was a map of the enormous holding tank of some kind, which she was now looking out into from beneath the surface. Without being consciously aware she was doing it, Joanne reached into her purse and took out her phone, having the mental capacity to make sure the flash was off for the camera application before she started to snap photographs of the room. She knew the chances of them showing anything but murky shadows were slim. However, she reasoned the warning on the door was there for a reason, and she had no desire to startle whatever dwelled in the tremendous artificial lake beyond. She walked to the glass, feeling incredibly small and insignificant. It was made of curved plexi-glass that followed perfectly the contour of the bowl. She reached out and laid a shaking hand on the plastic. It was cold to the touch, and for the second time in the last few minutes, she realised she was holding her breath as she stood there, basking in both the tranquillity of the scene before her and with a vague sense of danger. There was plainly a very good reason why this area was closed to the public, if only because she knew such a spectacular observation area would be a huge tourist attraction. For it to be closed to the public meant that the government had something that they didn't want people to see, which, as was her way, made her even more determined to find out what it was.

There was a clipboard hanging from a hook on the wall. She grabbed it, leafing through the papers, in between glances out the window into the murky greenish water. It looked to be a feeding schedule going back at least a couple of years. Occasionally, there were notes scrawled in the page margins in a hand that were difficult to read. One entry stood out on the front though.

90 feet! Fully Grown blue whale size!! WOW!

Blue whale.

She dropped the clipboard in disgust. As it was, she had a problem with corporations keeping dolphins and Orcas in captivity. Never did she expect the greedy, money hungry owners to try to house a blue whale, and a fully grown one at that, if the clipboard was to be believed. It was little wonder they had tried to keep it under cover. Public outrage would be off the scale if word got out that such a majestic and endangered creature was being held in the dark in the confines of a pool with no external stimulus. She knew all whales were social creatures that preferred to live in pods, not in solitude in a manmade pool. She couldn't understand why they had captured it if they plainly did not intend to display it to the public. She looked around the observation room, trying to gauge how much money it was costing to keep this particular area of the aquarium operational. A flush of hot anger raced through her when she considered that the poor whale was probably separated from its mother as a calf and brought here, confused and alone, until it was big enough to earn the owners of the aquarium a few more blood-covered dollars. The idea that she had worked there for so long and contributed to their lies, however unknowingly, made her nauseous. She re-opened her camera app, and began to snap pictures of the clipboard, particularly the entry relating to the Blue whale. It was as she was taking this photograph that something caught her eye, a sliver of movement from inside the tank.

She paused and looked out into the water, searching the undulating gloom. She was sure she had seen something, and yet, there was no movement at all, the pale greenish blue landscape deathly silent. She leaned closer, touching her nose to the cool Plexiglas. She strained her senses, eyes staring into the gloom, ears straining to hear even the smallest of sounds.

There.

She was certain she had seen it again, a dark smudge moving frustratingly just out of the periphery of her vision.

You're imagining things. Seeing what you want to see.

Maybe her inner voice was right. Then again, maybe it wasn't. She reasoned there must be *something* in the water. As good as the evidence was that she had gathered so far, it would pale in comparison to a shot of the actual captive whale. She waited, camera poised, breath held, watching for any sign of movement. It was as she realised just how still she was keeping that the message on the door floated back to her mind's eye, particularly the urgent way in which it was written.

OBSERVATION AREA
!!!WARNING!!!
NO MOVEMENT IN PRESENCE OF SUBJECT!
NO CAMERAS / MOBILE PHONES!
NO ARTIFICIAL LIGHT SOURCES!
NO ADMITTANCE WITHOUT PRIOR AUTHORISATION!

Why was it so urgent? Why all the exclamation points? She knew that whales in general were social creatures, despite their treatment at the hands of mankind. Even if she could understand the governments need to keep it a secret, the nature of the warning suggested the tank contained something more dangerous than the evidence suggested. There was a noise, although it didn't come from the water, but somewhere above her. The sound of a heavy door being opened. She waited and listened, and almost screamed when the dull rumble of an engine of some kind growled into life. Without wanting to wait around and risk being caught, and potentially having her camera confiscated, she hurried out of the observation area and back the way she had come. Had she waited just a few seconds longer, she would have seen the creature swim into view as it moved towards the winch operated by Andrews on the surface. She would have also, upon seeing the true nature of the creature, have reconsidered the decisions made in the following hours, which would lead to an eventual disastrous chain of events.

CHAPTER SIX

The pain of the hangovers didn't hurt anymore, at least not as much as having to look at his sorry reflection every day. To say the years had not been kind to Henry Rainwater was an understatement. He rolled onto his side, grunting as he sat up in his sagging bed, his feet kicking at the empty beer cans that seemed to swarm the floor. He rubbed his eyes, trying to ignore the involuntary shaking of his hands and the already desperate gnawing in his gut for more alcohol so he could blot out the coming day. It wasn't lost on him that he sat feeling sorry for himself and trying to ignore the stench of sweat and stale farts in his hovel of an apartment, or that he was a twenty eight year old man who looked ten years older, and felt even twenty years older than that. He rubbed at the white scar on his shoulder, the trophy of the bullet wound inflicted by Russo, which even now still hurt sometimes. Scratching at his unkempt beard, he reached over and grabbed his cigarettes from the bedside table. With hands still shaking, he lit up, and then dumped the overfull ashtray into the takeaway container on the floor, giving the half-eaten cheeseburger a dusting of grey ash. Inhaling deeply on his cancer stick, he tried to figure out how to best deal with the day. Laying a hand on his flabby stomach, he looked across the room to the dresser mirror, somehow managing mostly to ignore his own impish reflection and concentrating instead on the yellowed photograph and accompanying newspaper cutting taped to the glass. Although he couldn't quite read the headline, he had read it enough over the years to know it word for word.

LOCAL FISHERMAN WHO CHEATED DEATH DIES IN HEROIC RESCUE

Rainwater grunted, flicking ash absently to the floor. He looked at the photograph of Mackay, one of him as he should be remembered, a broad, loud voiced man, tough as nails, but warm and friendly. Better at least than Rainwaters last memory, which was of him sitting on the ice, holding the slick coils and contents of his stomach one hand, whilst he smoked a cigarette with the other. Unlike the photograph on the mirror, Rainwaters last image of Mackay was of a frightened man who knew death was coming to him no matter what he did, and there was nothing that could be done about it. In the end, he had been the hero, and had destroyed the giant sea creature in the Antarctic ice cave when he triggered an explosive charge that brought down the roof, and ensuring that the oceans remained safe.

Of course, the government made up their own story to explain Mackay's death, which made headline news in Alaska at least. The wider world had bigger things to worry about than a fisherman. Even so, the official account of what happened was, quite simply, bullshit. The article pinned next to Mackay's photo told a story of how Mackay made a solo rescue attempt on a stranded government vessel called the *Victorious*, and sadly drowned after saving all but two men, who also went down with the ship. For the government, it was a nice tidy story. They managed to explain away the deaths of Mackay, Russo, and Dexter, along with the sinking of the Victorious without fanfare or anyone being willing or able to prove otherwise.

Rainwater reached for the beer cans on the table, shaking each in turn and hoping to find liquid in one of them. At the third attempt, he got lucky, and although it felt like less than a third of a can, it would do. He held the can towards the picture on the wall.

"Happy anniversary, Mac," he slurred under his breath. "I'll never forget what you did for me."

With that, he drained the remainder of the cheap booze, wincing at the taste. Stifling a sour belch, he tossed the can on the floor with the others and took another drag on his cigarette. He knew he needed to make a change, to get himself clean and back on track. He hated the perpetual misery of his existence. Most of the time, he was able to forget it and bury his head in the sand. Today however - on the anniversary of Mackay's death - the guilt of how much of a mess he had made of his life after everything his friend had sacrificed was almost too much to handle. He promised himself he would do it. He would prove it to Mackay, and do his memory proud. He would get off the booze and get healthy. He would make his life one worth living.

Just not today.

Today was a bad day to try something so extreme. Today was a hard day.

Tomorrow.

Yes, he agreed with the weak voice in his head. Definitely tomorrow. A fresh start. A new beginning. Twenty four hours from now, he promised himself he would start on his journey to be a new man. First, though, he just needed a little drink, just something to take the edge off and help him to get through his day.

Just one. For Mackay.

Yes. Just one more drink, then tomorrow, he would do what he had to. Tomorrow, he would get clean.

II

Tom lived in an apartment complex close to the Florida Keys. The gated property was hardly extravagant, but it was his and that made all the difference. The rent was low, and it was close to where he worked. Joanne had used her key to let herself in whilst her boyfriend was at work, and was sitting at the computer showing Fernando and his friends the evidence from her late night trip into the restricted area of the aquarium.

"You're sure it's a blue whale?" Clayton said.

"No, I'm not sure at all. All I can show you is the photos I took. Either way, they're keeping something in there out of view of the public."

"So much for your sea monster," Marie said, nudging Clayton in the arm with her elbow.

Fernando looked at them, jealous of how close they were standing, and how little either seemed to mind that their skin was touching. "Whatever it is, it's not right that they're keeping it captive."

"Tell me about it," Joanne said, turning away from the computer screen. "It was awful in there. Those conditions were appalling. The poor thing must never have seen daylight."

"Maybe we should tell someone. The police maybe?" Marie said.

"No, that won't help. It would just drag on for years like the SeaWorld protests. Something needs to be done now. If this is a

Blue Whale, it needs to be freed," Joanne said, just as angry as she had been the night before. She was about to say more when the apartment door opened and was slammed closed. Tom strode across the room, glaring at his brother.

"What's going on? Why aren't you at work?" Joanne said.

"I got fired thanks to my little shit of a brother," Tom said as he dropped down into the chair by the window.

"They can't do that! Why fire you?" She replied, crossing the room to sit on the armrest of the chair and hugging him.

"Because, when the new security team went back through the systems, they figured out he used my key card to access the building when him and his pals decided it would be a good idea to break in. Gross negligence they said. It apparently put them in a position where they had no choice but to let me go."

"So they know who we are now?" Jim said.

"No, for some reason I covered for you all. They think my card was stolen, but they still say I was responsible for losing it in the first place."

"Sorry, man, I had no idea-"

"Don't even bother," Tom snapped. "As always, you do stupid shit without thinking of the consequences. This is why mom and dad couldn't cope with you."

"Fuck you, Tom," Fernando shot back, not wanting to be embarrassed in front of his friends. "If you hadn't left it lying around, I wouldn't have been able to take it."

"You're seriously trying to blame me for this? For leaving my own stuff in my own house without thinking of hiding it away from you and your stupid fucking friends?" Tom hissed, glaring at his brother.

"They didn't know I took it. Hell, we didn't even know that we were even going to try to get in until we got to talking on the beach."

"Let me guess, another day wasted getting drunk whilst the rest of us go to work. Why the hell don't you just get a job like everyone else?"

"It's summer break. Pretty soon, I'll be going to college. Jesus, Tom, don't be such a bitch about this. You hated that job anyway."

"That doesn't mean I didn't need it. It's all right for you. You still live at home and seem quite happy to let our parents pay your way. It's different in the real world. There are bills to pay, not to mention rent, food, and the countless other things that exist outside your little dream world. We can't all sit around on the beach all day watching the world go by."

"Who the hell are you to judge me?" Fernando fired back as his friends looked on. "You're not perfect you know."

"Look, this isn't helping," Joanne said, hoping to diffuse the coming argument. "You both need to calm down and take a breath."

Reluctantly, they did as they were told, Fernando returning to his seat and ignoring the smirk from Clayton as he passed him.

"Anyway," Tom said as he removed his tie, "what the hell are you all doing here in my soon to be former apartment?"

Nobody said anything at first. Instead, they all looked to Joanne, knowing that she would be the best intermediary between them and Tom, and the one who would have the best chance of making him listen to what had happened.

"There's something we need to tell you, and when you hear it, you just might be glad you don't work at that place anymore."

"I don't like the sound of this," he muttered.

For the next ten minutes, Joanne explained the situation and showed Tom the photographs she had taken. Fernando was sure he would walk out or call them idiots at any point, and yet, the outburst never came. Instead, he listened and let them finish.

"So, what do you think?" Joanne asked.

"This is old news, or at least to me it is. That holding tank has been there since the place opened."

"You knew about it?" Joanne said.

"I knew it was back there, after all, I work security. At least I did. We were always told it was a, uh, what was the word they used," he frowned, searching his memory, "observation pool. All part of the next stage of the opening of the aquarium apparently. No big deal."

"You don't think it's a little weird?"

"Are you kidding?" Tom said, managing a smile. "That entire place is weird. Even though I was on security, there are parts of the building that were always locked. Doors with keypads on them, which nobody seems to know the numbers to, plus all the people who come and go that aren't part of the official staff list or have official job titles. Come on, babe, you work there, you must have seen it."

"I only saw the gift shop and the staff room. It's not something I ever knew about. How come you never said anything before?"

"I don't really know," he said with a shrug. "I never really linked it to anything sinister. All I was concerned with was keeping my job, which actually makes what happened this morning seem a little bit easier to understand."

"What do you mean?" Joanne asked.

"This morning, the new security teams were due on site in response to the break in. My job was to coordinate them, set them up, and show them the ropes. Usually, my patrol route only allows me on the walkway above that lagoon, and only at certain times of day, it's always been that way. Anyway, old Harry had been on his patrol during the night shift and had lost his radio somewhere on his patrol. It's an instant dismissal, and because the two of us were already in the shit for our slow response to the break in, I offered to go look for it for him to make sure the new guys didn't have anything to report to Mr Andrews. Harry thought he might have left it in one of the labs near where I caught you all trying to break in. Apparently, he'd stopped for a breather and to give his legs a rest. Anyway, I went up there to look for it and there it was, just sitting on the table. If I'd just turned back then and gone back to my station, I might still have a job. Instead, my curiosity got the better of me."

"What did you see?" Fernando asked.

"Well, usually, the lagoon is in darkness when I patrol. They have lights aimed at the windows up there so you can never really see down below because of the glare. This time though, there were no lights. Probably because I wasn't supposed to be in there as it was outside of the designated patrol times. Anyways, there are all these people rigging all this equipment up around the edge of the water."

"Like what?" Joanne asked.

"Cranes. Lifting equipment. Heavy duty stuff too. Seems to me your little adventure has the people in charge spooked. Looks like they're planning to move this whale of yours."

"Move it? Where? How?" Joanne asked.

"Hell, I don't know. They saw me and gestured for me to move on. Ten minutes later, I'm pulled into the supervisor's office and told I was being let go because of this whole key card thing. Bastards."

"Seems to me like you saw more than you were supposed to," Clayton muttered.

"Either way, it's best left alone. Whatever they're up to, it's obviously way bigger than us."

"Could they be returning it to the wild?" Marie said, giving another of those flirtatious glances towards Clayton.

"Doubt it," Tom replied. "They spent a small fortune on keeping that area secure for a reason. I can't see them just throwing away whatever is in there just because my dumb shit of a brother decided it would be fun to break in," he said, winking at his sibling who replied with a half-smile.

"Why don't we do it for them?"

It was the first thing Jim had said since Tom had come home. They looked at him, pretending not to notice the fresh bruise under his eye, which everyone knew had come at the hands of his father.

"What do you mean?" Fernando asked.

"You're all keen to see this thing freed. Why don't you take matters into your own hands?"

"I don't see how we can do anything about it," Clayton said, his usual self-confidence surprisingly absent. "Besides, I thought you were trying to keep out of trouble?"

Jim didn't reply to Clayton. Instead, he looked directly at Tom. "You seem pretty certain they plan to move this thing sometime soon, right?"

"Yeah, it looked that way," Tom replied, not liking where the conversation was going.

"Then, why don't we wait until it's in transit, intercept the transport, and get this fish back in the water where it belongs."

"That's insane," Tom said, hoping Jim was joking. "As much as I'm against animal cruelty, I'm not about to go to jail over it. What you're talking about is not only dumb, it's also highly illegal."

"Come on," Jim said, the glimmer in his eyes telling the rest of the group just how serious he was, "you've seen those video clips of Greenpeace protesters fucking with the Japs about the whaling they do. All they ever get is a slap on the wrists because the governments know it would look bad to prosecute someone for doing the right thing."

"This is different to spraying a whaler with a hose," Tom countered. "You're taking about stealing a truck, and then the logistics of trying actually to get the whale back in the water without killing or hurting it. It would be impossible."

"No, I'm talking about borrowing a truck for a few minutes. I don't deny it would be hard, but I still think we could do it."

"Come on," Tom said to the rest of the group. "Will one of you help me out here? Have you heard this crap?"

"Let's hear him out," Fernando said.

"Are you crazy?"

"I wanna hear it too," Joanne said, holding Toms hand.

"You're all insane," Tom muttered, pulling his hand away and sitting back in his seat, arms folded.

Jim waited for a few seconds, and then went on. "Chances are, they will need a big ass flatbed to transport this thing. According to those photos, this thing is 90 feet long. That means they will need a specialist truck driver to drive this whale wherever they intend to take it. All we need to do is pull him over, and convince him to get out, and then take over the vehicle."

"And who do you think will drive it?" Tom said.

"I will," Jim fired back with a grin. "I'll also convince the driver that it's in his interest to just jump out and let us get on with what we need to do."

"This won't work," Marie said, her brow furrowed, "it's too risky."

"Finally, a voice of reason," Tom said.

"Not really," Clayton cut in. "It seems risky because it's an extreme move, but imagine the public response if we pull this off. How the hell could they arrest us? What would we have done wrong?"

"They would lock us up and throw away the key," Tom grunted. "I can't believe you're all even discussing this."

"No, they wouldn't."

"How do you reach that conclusion?"

"Think about it," Jim said with a grin, "you're seeing things from a 'them and us' perspective. Look at it how the media will see it. To them, we will have bravely liberated a fully-grown blue whale and returned it to the ocean, free from a life of misery and darkness at the hands of the government. We'll be heroes. Public pressure will make all the difference."

"You know, he's right," Fernando said, "I think we could do this."

"For God's sake, listen to what you're saying. This is insane."

"Actually, I agree," Joanne said, looking at Tom. "We can't just sit and watch this happen."

"I can't believe this from you of all people. This isn't just a game. People could be hurt."

"This animal is already hurt. I thought you knew me well enough to know how strongly I feel about things like this."

"I know you feel strongly, baby, I really do, it's just this is too much. It's a bad idea."

"You know, it's attitudes like that which stops change from happening in this world. Too many people are willing to sit back and let somebody else make the big decisions that really make a difference."

"I don't want to see you get hurt, any of you," Tom said.

"It will hurt me more if we don't do anything about this," Joanne replied.

"You can't put me in this kind of a position. You can't expect me just to go along with this."

"Do you love me?" She asked.

"Of course I do. You know I do."

"And I love you too. Because of that, I'd never force you to do something you don't want to do. At the same time, I don't expect you to try to stop me from doing something I really believe in."

"You see the position I'm in here? This is impossible. Can't you see the risk? Can't you understand the trouble you'll be in if this goes wrong?"

"Sometimes, risk is worthwhile. Sometimes, those who risk really make the difference. I won't force you to do anything," she said, reaching out and again taking his hands in hers. "I would rather do something like this with you, than without you."

Tom looked at the others, who apart from Marie, seemed just as determined. "You understand that if you do this, it could change things forever. We don't know the whole story here. We don't know why they have that thing held."

"It's not their right to keep it. Whatever reason they think they have, it's unjustified. That poor whale belongs in the ocean. It deserves to be free."

"What if it costs us our freedom? What if we all end up in jail?" He replied.

"That's a risk I'm prepared to take," Joanne replied. "Will you help us?"

Tom looked at them all, wondering just how things had managed to escalate into madness so quickly. For as much as he was sure it was a mistake, he hated the idea of letting Joanne down more than listening to his own rationale, which was telling him that nothing good could come from Jim's plan. On the other side of the coin, he felt betrayed by his employers, people he had worked for without complaint for a long time, and who had seen fit to sweep him aside without a second thought. It was this and his love for Joanne that made him ignore his better judgement and agree to help.

III

Cutlery clanked against plates as people made polite chat over dinner. Neil Barker squirmed in his seat and adjusted his tie, then checked his watch again. His host was now twenty minutes late, and Barker was starting to get agitated. He looked around the room as he sat alone at his table and tried to estimate how much wealth was sitting around him. He wouldn't be surprised if many of the dishes served here would cost the equivalent of a month's wages for him. At least the water was free though. He picked up his glass and took a sip as one of the ever present waiters hovered nearby like an agitated fly, wondering why this man who was clearly too poor to eat in such an establishment was sitting and taking up valuable table space. It was only the name the reservation was booked under that stopped the inevitable questioning and pestering to leave, because as unable to afford to dine in such a restaurant as Neil was, the man he was meeting was more than able to.

Someone approached his table, a dark skinned man in a sharp

black suit and impeccably parted hair of the same colour. Neil suspected he might have been wrong, and this was the restaurant manager approaching to tell him the restaurant was getting full and was incredibly busy, and that he might like to consider moving on and allowing someone else to be seated. To Neil's surprise, the man said none of these things. Instead, he took a seat at the opposite side of the table.

"Can I help you?" Barker said.

"We had an appointment."

"My appointment wasn't with you."

"Mr Decker sent me," the man said.

"And you are?"

"My name doesn't matter, Mr Barker."

"Still, I was supposed to meet Mr Decker. This is highly unusual."

"Mr Decker is in Dubai on business. He sends his apologies," the man said, just about managing an almost sincere smile.

"This is a sensitive subject, I need to speak to him personally."

"I'm fully aware of the creature, Mr Barker. I'm also fully aware of the agreement in place between yourself and the Decker foundation. What I, and Mr Decker don't understand, is why it is taking so long to achieve the results you promised."

"Look," Barker said, lowering his voice, "it's not that easy. You think I want to delay this?"

"No, Mr Decker knows you're trying your best. He also knows that you are more than interested in securing your fee. I believe it was ten million?"

Barker squirmed and looked around the restaurant. Nobody was paying the slightest bit of attention. "Look, I was hoping to speak directly to Mr Decker, but as it seems you know all about this, you'll have to do."

"Go on," the man said, folding his hands on the desk.

"They're moving the creature."

For the first time, the mystery man seemed rattled. It only lasted for a second, but Barker saw the shadow of uncertainty pass over his face. "What exactly do you mean?"

"I mean what I said. Some stupid kids broke into the facility. They didn't see anything and security chased them off. Either way, my bosses are spooked. I tried to buy more time to complete the cloning process, but they're going ahead with moving it."

"When?" The man said, now all business and leaning slightly closer to Barker.

"A couple of days. A week maximum. Government is shipping it out to some top secret facility."

"I hope for your sake you have a backup plan."

"Of course," Barker said, ignoring the veiled threat. "I have the next best thing. I'll even drop my fee by fifty percent for the inconvenience caused."

The man smiled and leaned back in his chair. "Go on."

"No," Barker said. "The rest I speak directly to Mr Decker about. No offence."

"Mr Decker is a very busy man."

"I'm sure he'll find time. Tell him to call me if he wants to know what my offer is. It will only stay open for a limited time. As soon as the creature is relocated, I'll be moving onto a new project."

"Nothing as exciting as this I expect."

"It might be, actually. Some military genetics program called Project Apex. Either way, I'm booked in to fly over to Washington to be briefed on this at the weekend. This is a time critical situation."

"I'll make sure Mr Decker is made aware of the urgency. I also need to know if your counter proposal is worth his while. As you know, Mr Decker is incredibly passionate about this."

"But not enough to come here and meet me himself," Barker grunted as he took a drink of his water.

"Touché."

Barker stood and loosened his tie. "Have him call me. Trust me, it will be worth his while."

"The limo," the man said as Barker walked past him.

"Say again?"

"Go to the limo outside. Mr Decker is in it."

"Then why the hell didn't he come in and meet me?"

"He doesn't like to eat here. Go to him now. Give him your proposal."

Barker nodded. Ignoring the butterflies swirling in his stomach, he made his way outside.

CHAPTER SEVEN

Sam Bolton had always wanted to be a truck driver. Ever since his father gave him his first toy big rig as a child, he knew driving one was what he wanted to do with the rest of his life. Unlike most childhood dreams, it was one, which didn't fade. Now with over thirty years' experience behind him, he was a long haul veteran. He had done it all. Ice road trucking in Canada, which involved transporting goods across frozen lakes to remote locations in sub-zero conditions, to navigating the Yungas Road in Bolivia, which was a real test of guts or insanity. With a cliff face on one side and a sheer three hundred foot drop to certain death on the other, it took both nerves and accuracy to navigate. Even so, every once in a while, something new and unexpected came up such as this most recent job. He had done a little animal transportation before, but that was mostly sheep or other livestock, certainly nothing of this scale. He was driving a customised flatbed rig with a 100 foot long trailer. With two extra axles to help drive the vehicle along, it boasted twenty six wheels and twelve foot side fences down the full length of the bed, which were covered by a hard plastic shell. Heavy and cumbersome even without cargo, it required a deft hand to pilot. Bolton reversed the trailer down the loading bay of the ocean world aquarium, guided in by men in high visibility jackets. Once inside, he shut off the engine, tied his long grey hair into a ponytail, slipped on his tattered green baseball cap, and climbed out of the cab, grateful to be able to stretch his legs.

"Who's in charge here?" He grunted to one of the men who had guided him in.

"I am," Andrews replied, striding to meet Bolton.

Sam handed over the paperwork and looked at the immense bowl like aquarium. "So, what exactly is the cargo?"

"Marine life. Whale to be precise. For transportation down to Tampa."

"Whale huh," Bolton said, taking another look at the aquarium holding tank. "You know, I just drive the thing. I ain't responsible for makin' sure it survives the trip."

"There will be a team riding along with the creature in the back, hence the side fences."

"How many?"

"Just four."

"Same story with them. I drive the truck. If their ass falls out because they ain't paying attention, it ain't my fault."

"We understand that," Andrews snapped. "Just make sure you arrive safely in Tampa. This cargo is incredibly valuable."

"Your fish will be safe enough. Pretty straight shot all the way from here to Tampa. Good thing too. Turning this rig is a bitch. If I were you, I'd be more worried about this heat."

"The whale will be covered in a wet wrap. My team also have water tanks which will be loaded on to the truck. They'll keep the animal cool and moist."

Bolton nodded. "How much does she weigh?"

"She's big. Around two hundred and twenty thousand pounds."

Bolton whistled through his teeth. "What's that, a hundred tons or more?"

"Around one-ten."

"With all that weight, you sure this fish of yours will survive the trip?"

"We have a harness. It's supported and reinforced to take the weight off her in transit. We're confident she will survive the move."

"That's all up to you," Bolton said with a half-smile. "All I get paid to do is drive the truck. Is there somewhere I can grab a bite to eat till' you load her up?"

"Staff restaurant. I'll show you where it is." Andrews replied, finally giving in to the nerves at what they were about to do. As he led the truck driver towards the public area of the aquarium, he gave a glance to the cranes, which had been shipped in overnight, already modified to handle the bulk of the creature. If there had been any doubt before, Andrews knew for certain that Tomlinson had been planning to move the animal, and was just waiting for the first chance to justify it. There was no other explanation as to how they had managed to deliver the required equipment so quickly. Not unlike his many dealings with Russo when they first captured the creature, Andrews couldn't shake the feeling in his gut that something was going to happen. It was the same thing police officers called their sixth sense, an absolute knowledge that the shit was about to hit the fan, and when it did, it would lead to nothing but trouble for everyone.

II

Clara's apartment was lavish and decadent, which was something the version of herself from five years earlier, would have scoffed and shaken her head at. This Clara though, had buried the old version of herself in the past and had grown content to live in a world of polished marble and overpriced furniture. As far as masks went, she wore it well. One thing she couldn't hide behind her expensive makeup, designer clothes, and bleach whitened teeth, was her creativity, or in this case, lack of. She was sitting at her desk, staring at the blinking cursor with no clue of what to write or how to do it.

Writing the first book had been easy, almost a therapeutic exercise as she recounted what had happened to her in real life, and changing just enough to push it into the realms of fiction. She had changed names but not characters, locations but not events. Of course, the government got wind of what she was doing and did everything they could to stop her. She had, however, gambled (rightly) on the fact that they would stop short of actually taking action for the simple reason that it was in their best interests not to have the general public digging into why they were so interested in the story. As far as burials go, the actual facts about what happened five years earlier had been expertly covered up. Dexter's murder had been turned into an accidental death at sea. Russo's existence had been deleted completely, which to her was frustrating as it meant that the slimy, jittery government agent had gotten away with his crimes even in death. Without warning, she saw him in her mind's eye, those deep, penetrating eyes, which felt as if they were staring straight through you. Even though he was long dead, the thought of him was still frightening, so much so that in her fictional retelling of the story, Russo had been replaced by a much tamer, less intensely cruel man. Her agent had suggested as a villain he was perhaps too nice, and even though there were numerous requests to beef up the evil scale, Clara had refused. She couldn't tell her agent why, but even in the realms of fiction, Russo was too far off the scale to justify bringing back to life in print.

There was never any expectation from the book, no real plans to try to sell it at first. She had written it mostly as a means to cope, to get the events out of her mind and onto paper in the hope of exorcising the demons. For the most part, it had worked, and had allowed her to resume some sense of normality. It was only when she showed a few pages to a friend that things changed. Blown away by the opening chapters, Clara's friend had pressed her to send a copy to a literary agent friend of hers. Again, with no expectation of anything, Clara went along with it, posting a copy of the manuscript and promptly forgetting all about it. A month or so later, she received a call back from the agent with news that if she signed with them, they could secure a lucrative contract with a publisher who was interested in publishing the book.

Had she known the attention it would get, she might have declined. Now though, it was too late to turn back, and although it had made her an incredibly wealthy woman, it still hadn't made her happy.

Turning away from the blinking cursor on screen, she picked up her phone and navigated to the address book, scrolling to Rainwater's number and hesitating, wondering why she still had it after all this time. Her thumb hovered over the dial button, wishing she could just speak to him to ask his advice.

No.

Not after what happened. Those bridges are long burned, and the modern day versions of Rainwater and herself were worlds apart from the ones that met five years earlier. With a sigh, she put the phone on the desk and returned her attention to the screen.

CHAPTER EIGHT

Clayton shifted in the front seat of the pickup, unsure if he was more nervous or excited. He decided it was the former, and looked out the window as traffic rolled past them.

"Take it easy," Jim said from the passenger side, one arm hanging nonchalantly out of the window. "Smoke?"

Clayton took the offered cigarette, lighting up and blowing smoke out the open window. "I don't like this."

"We agreed. It's all worked out."

"What if something goes wrong? We can't plan for everything."

"Trust me, I know what I'm doing."

Clayton nodded. The fact that Jim seemed so comfortable was part of the problem. For as much as they were friends, Clayton knew he was known to get volatile and unpredictable. It was something he had wanted to approach more than once in the past, yet, hadn't because he was a little bit afraid of the reaction it might receive. Checking his phone again, he shifted position and tried to push his negativity away.

"So," Jim said with a grin, "you and Marie. What's the story there?"

"Nothin' to tell."

"Come on, don't give me that shit. I've seen the way she gives you the eye."

"Like I said, nothing to tell."

"Yeah, I bet," Jim snorted. "What happened? She knock you back?"

"Come on, knock it off," Clayton snapped.

"Jesus, relax, I was just screwin' around."

Clayton didn't answer, and checked his phone again. Jim watched, an amused grin stretched across his face. "She said she'd call when the truck was on its way."

"I still don't know how we're going to do this. We don't even know if the driver will get out of the truck."

"He will."

"What makes you so sure?"

Jim grinned, the expression making Claytons heart plummet into his shoes. Jim reached into the glove box and pulled out a rag. Even before it was unwrapped, Clayton knew what it was.

"No, absolutely not," Clayton said as Jim revealed the handgun.

"Come on, it's just so we can intimidate the guy into giving up the truck."

"Screw this, man. Helping to free this whale is one thing. Guns are something else. I won't have any part of it."

Clayton started the engine, intending to drive to the meeting point where they were to pick up the others.

"Shut it off," Jim said.

Clayton froze. His friend was still grinning, but the sightless eye of the gun was trained on Clayton from the passenger side.

"Are you fucking insane?" Clayton hissed, his fear masquerading as anger.

"Relax, I'm not gonna shoot you. Look." He pulled the trigger, causing Clayton to flinch away. The gun clicked harmlessly. "Fuckin' things empty."

"That's not the point. This is too much. We're getting in way over our heads here."

"You won't be saying that when it's done. When this fish is free, me and you will be the heroes," he said, widening his grin.

"Heroes to who?"

"The rest of the group. We'll be legends."

Clayton turned away and looked out the window. The grin on his friend's face was starting to scare him. He was trying to think of ways to get out of what they were about to do when his phone vibrated. Watched by Jim, Clayton picked up the handset. "It's time," he said, flicking another glance in the direction of the handgun in Jim's lap.

"Good," Jim said, looking more agitated. "Just follow my lead and everything will go down smooth. Trust me."

Clayton nodded, and then despite the nausea racing through him, he started the engine and pulled off the hard shoulder and into traffic.

II

Fully loaded with its cargo, the specially designed flatbed truck was hard to control even for its experienced driver. Even the minute adjustments to allow for the contours of the road were slow and had to be pre-empted. For a lesser driver, it would have been easy to overcompensate and slew off the road. Sam Bolton, however, was masterful as he shifted into high gear. As instructed, he kept to a safe speed, keeping the journey as smooth as he could. Even on the straight, flat route, the engine was struggling to haul its massive load. He hadn't been allowed to see the creature, and it had already been loaded onto his vehicle when he returned from his overpriced lunch in the aquarium restaurant, which suited him fine.

He shifted into a lower gear as the road inclined slightly, balancing the throttle, careful not to go too fast. For the first time in years, he was feeling nervous, and had to give every ounce of his concentration to the road ahead. The oncoming traffic rubbernecked as they passed, unused to seeing such a huge vehicle on the roads, especially one with such a mysterious cargo. Normally, such a vehicle would require a police escort. However, due to the covert nature of the operation, it had been deemed both inappropriate and something that would potentially raise too many questions.

He smiled at the thought, wondering how many children had passed coming in the opposite direction in the back of cars driven by parents perhaps heading to the coast for a holiday, and upon seeing the truck, had decided they wanted to drive one someday too, just the way he had. It was because he was thinking of this that he didn't immediately notice the rusty white pickup truck ahead swerve into his lane, and put itself on a collision course with the trailer.

A less experienced driver would have slammed on the brakes, and in doing so, risk the rear trailer fishtailing and tipping, spilling cargo and people riding along with it all over the road. Instead, he gently pumped them, feeling for the signs of locking up and releasing the pressure for a second, in effect, performing as a manual anti-lock brake. His can of coke spilled over into the foot well, followed by the mountain of newspapers on the passenger seat. Neither of those were his concern though. His only thought was of safely bringing the truck to a halt. With a shudder and groan of brakes, the forward momentum of the truck ceased, and it hissed to a pneumatic halt.

Seconds later, the pickup did the same. Bolton watched as two balaclava-clad men threw open the doors and climbed out, racing for the driver's side door. At first, Bolton wondered if they had spotted something, some emergency that required his attention. It was only when he saw the handgun that he realised something else was happening.

"Get out of the truck right now, motherfucker!" the one with gun screamed whilst his colleague fidgeted beside him and threw concerned glances at the traffic who weren't stopping and getting involved in the situation.

"What the hell are you doing?" Bolton said, half opening the door.

"Get the fuck out," Jim screamed, waving the gun for emphasis.

"Alright, take it easy," Bolton said, clambering down out of the cab.

He could tell they were just kids, and the one without the gun wasn't really certain of his actions, which made his next decision easier to make. He lunged for the one with the weapon, sure that if he could disarm him, his friend would give up.

"Hey, back up, back up-" Jim squealed as Bolton grappled with him, trying to pry the weapon free. Clayton looked on, absolutely numb and unable to react. It was the worst possible scenario. His instinct told him to run, yet, he couldn't leave his friend, as seemingly off the rails as he was. The entire inner conflict was rendered useless, when the crisp sound of a single gunshot rolled through the air as the driver of the rig fell to the ground.

III

There was no fear. No panic. Jim looked down at the old man lying in the road, blood welling up from the wound in his stomach and he wasn't really sure what he felt. All he knew was they had come too far to go back.

"What did you do? What the fuck did you do?" Clayton screeched from somewhere behind him.

Jim didn't hear it. He was mesmerised in watching the old man as he lay dying.

"You said it wasn't loaded, you said it was just supposed to scare him," Clayton hissed.

Jim watched as the man took a last gasping breath, and then stopped, eyes staring blankly into the crisp blue sky.

"Get in the truck," Jim said, his voice cold and commanding.

Too afraid to do anything but comply, Clayton did as he was told; glad Jim couldn't see him crying under his balaclava. He clambered up into the passenger side, feeling like he was a stranger living in somebody else's body. Jim climbed into the driver's side and closed the door, pulling off his balaclava. Unlike Clayton who was still coming to terms with what had happened, Jim was grinning.

"Let's get this show on the road," he said, slipping the truck into gear and setting off, nudging Jim's beaten pickup aside and leaving the dead driver by the roadside. Cars were pulling to a stop now to see if they could help. Jim picked up speed, arms hacking at the wheel as he struggled to control the truck.

"This fucker's heavy," he muttered.

Clayton didn't answer. Instead, he pulled off his balaclava and stared out of the window.

"Hey, I'm talking to you," Jim said.

"You killed that man back there," Clayton croaked.

"It wasn't my fault. He should have done as I told him. Anyway, we don't know he's dead for sure."

"We watched him die!" Clayton screamed.

"Shut up, we don't know for sure. He might have just passed out or something."

"We're gonna go down for this, Jim. Both of us. Don't you realise what you've done? This isn't something petty like shoplifting or carjacking. This is murder."

"Relax; it will never come to that," Jim said, trying to convince himself just as much as Clayton. "Besides, nobody knows who we are. Nobody knows what we've done."

"Your truck is at the scene!" Clayton said, slamming his fist on the dash. "They can link it to you. They'll hunt you down for murder, Jim. You've crossed the line. You can't go back now."

A cloud of uncertainty passed over Jim's face. Clayton watched as his friend came to terms with the reality of the situation. "Well, it might be okay," he said, barely able to muster any conviction. "Like I said, he might just be wounded. It might be alright. Besides, it never would have happened if he hadn't gone for the gun. I mean, who the hell does something like that?"

"Why did you load it?" Clayton asked quietly.

"I don't know," Jim shrugged as he pulled off his mask. "I was thinkin' maybe I could intimidate the guy if he didn't go along with it. I was gonna fire a shot into the air, scare him a little, like they do in the movies, you know? Then the old prick came at me and things got out of hand. Hell, you were there, you saw it. You can vouch for me, right Clayton?"

"You need to turn yourself in. We need to stop the truck right now and you need to give yourself up. The longer you run, the worse you'll make things for yourself."

"Then I'll have done this for nothing. At least if we do this, they'll see why, they'll see the reason. That will help my case, won't it?"

Clayton hated the pleading tone in Jim's voice almost as much as the waxy tone of his skin and desperate set of his grin.

"Yeah, Maybe," Clayton mumbled, choosing his words carefully. For as much as he didn't think Jim would hurt him, he also didn't expect him to have ever gone as far as shooting a man for no reason. Either way, it was plain to see that he was a man with nothing to lose, and he knew well enough that desperate men do desperate things when they have to.

"Promise me you won't tell the others what happened."

Clayton looked at his friend, trying to see past the desperation. "They'll find out soon enough, this will be all over the news. You can't hide this from them."

"I know that, but don't make this all for nothing. As soon as we get this thing back in the water, I'll turn myself in. Explain how it was an accident. How nobody else was involved."

"Okay, good idea," Clayton said, not having the heart to tell Jim that freeing a blue whale wasn't going to hold water and give him any kind of a free pass against a murder charge, no matter what the initial intention was.

"Let's just hope the others are ready for us," Jim said as he wrestled with the wheel, changing direction and heading up the up the Florida coast. In the back, Andrews's staff stayed in position through a combination of fear and sense of duty to the creature. They could ony stay as helpless passengers as the truck rumbled closer to its destination.

IV

Minutemen Causeway,
Cocoa Beach, Florida.

Fernando, Emma, and Tom, waited on the beach, each nervous and excited in equal measure. Already the golden sands of Cocoa Beach were filling with people, which meant they would have quite a crowd for their planned operation. Tom paced, kicking sand whilst his brother and Emma stood nearby, trying not to look like they were up to no good.

They had chosen Cocoa Beach as the best place to return the whale to the sea, for the simple reason that it was possible to drive the truck directly from the road onto the sand and have enough space to get the trailer into the water. As far as freeing the whale itself went, the plan was simple in principal. Jim had been instructed to drive straight down the beach, wait for them to get in the back, usher out the team who were riding along to keep the whale moist, and then cut it loose from its harness. Jim would then reverse the truck into the ocean until the natural buoyancy of the water allowed the whale to swim free. There was risk involved of course. The stress to the creature would be a telling factor. However, they were way too far in now to change their minds, and so were hoping for a minor miracle. Their job upon seeing the truck arrive at the beach was to clear the way and ensure clear passage to the water.

They heard it before they saw it, a throaty rumble which punctuated the pleasant sound of surf on sand. They watched as it came, chrome grille shimmering in the sunlight, the sheer size of the truck overwhelming. For Fernando, it was a revelation. It was finally real. It was finally happening. He glanced towards Marie, and was surprised to find her looking back, small smile on her face.

They were about to take part in something spectacular.

In the truck, Jim levelled off and pointed the vehicle towards the beach. The passed shops and storefronts selling beachwear and drinks. People stopped to stare as Jim increased his speed. Ahead, the road faded into sandy beach, and beyond that, the ocean gently rolled. He could see the others ushering people aside, making them move to allow the truck through. To ensure their compliance, he honked the horn, an incessant noise as he floored the accelerator.

Because of the weight of the cargo, it was necessary to approach at speed. If Jim slowed, the wheels would bog down and they would lose forward momentum. The harder, more compacted sand at the water's edge, would with luck, give them enough grip to do what needed to be done.

"You might wanna hold on," Jim said, as they approached the transition between asphalt and sand.

The truck jolted and groaned, almost slewing out of control. From the cab, Clayton and Jim could feel the truck struggle to retain its momentum as the road surface changed, throwing up great clouds of sand in its wake, as it edged towards the water.

"Faster, you need to speed up," Clayton said as they bumped along.

"I'm doin' the best I can," Jim grunted through gritted teeth.

Just when it seemed like they would bog down and be stuck, the texture under them changed again as they reached the wetter, more compacted sand. Suddenly, finding grip, the truck lurched forward, then slewed to the right. Even for an experienced driver, there would have been little chance of correcting the slide. For a complete novice like Jim, there was no hope at all. The truck powered into the water, its trailer jack knifing after it. In the back, the creature was slammed against the inner wall, crushing three of its handlers against the iron railing and killing them instantly. The shift in momentum threw the trailer side on into the water until its wheels found purchase in the sand and tipped the entire truck, trailer, and all on its side, half submerging it in water.

"Holy shit," Tom said as he charged into the water, leaping in and swimming to help, swiftly followed by Fernando.

Inside the cab, Clayton's scream had been cut off by the

seawater that flooded in through the open window mere seconds before he was thrown against the interior of the cab. Jim was also thrown out of his seat into the water filled passenger side of the cab, clashing heads with Clayton on the way. Dazed and confused, freedom looked a long way away from where they bobbed in the water, looking up into the blue square of light above them from the driver's side window.

Outside, Fernando and Tom were in nine feet of water looking for a way to get into the cab. They swam to the front window, peering inside to their friends. Tom knocked on the glass, relieved to see both Clayton and Tom give the thumbs up.

"We need to get them out of there. See if you can break the glass," Fernando said as he kicked to stay afloat.

Tom did as he was asked, kicking at the glass as best he could whilst treading water. "I can't get enough momentum. We need to get something to break it in, we need to-"

The trailer moved, jerking a full two feet deeper into the water and dragging the cab with it as its cargo started to wake from the effects of the sedation.

"What the fuck?" Fernando said, swimming towards the cab.

"Whale must be trying to get loose."

As if in direct response, the truck slid a further foot and a half towards deeper water. In the cab, Clayton and Jim started to panic as the water level rose.

Tom turned towards the dozen or so beach goers who were wading out to help. "Call the Coast Guard or something. My friends are trapped in here."

In the back of the trailer, the creature stirred as it overcame the effects of the sedative, its senses overwhelmed by the array of scents from the open ocean, sensations that were new and incredibly stimulating after a life in captivity. The creature lay half submerged in the water, only held afloat by its damaged support harness, which had saved it from certain death during the crash. Once again, it shoved against its restraints, dragging trailer, cab, and all, further into the ocean, its harness groaning in protest as one of the creature's thick tentacles came free, pushing aside the floating corpses of its dead handlers. The two who were lucky enough not to have been crushed by the creature, scrambled out of the back into the water, swimming for the beach as quickly as they could. Unlike the growing crowds, they were fully aware that the cargo wasn't a whale, even if that was the word spreading around the people gathering at the scene.

"What the hell's happening?" Jim said as the water level rose.

"It's the whale, it's pulling us deeper."

"Then let's get the hell out of here," Jim replied.

"Agreed. Give me a boost up."

Jim helped Clayton to clamber up the vertical inside of the cab. He managed to grab the steering wheel and pull himself clear of the water. "Alright, I'm gonna try climb up the driver's seat and out."

"What about me?"

"Once I'm up there, I can kick out the window and pull you up."

Jim nodded, treading water and hanging on the edge of the submerged passenger side seat.

"Okay, here goes."

Clayton swung towards the seat, managing to hook his foot onto it. He clambered up, putting one foot on the inner edge of the steering wheel and the other between seat and backrest, as he reached for the door handle directly above him. At the same time, the creature detected a plethora of signals from the coastal waters that were teeming with life of all kinds. Its senses overwhelmed by the masses of data, it lunged and thrashed, desperate to free itself and explore its new environment as its movements dragged the trailer even deeper into the water. Clayton was thrown back into the cab, hooking his foot through the steering wheel on the way down, his ankle snapping with explosive agony as his upper half went under water. He thrashed in a panic, unable to free himself or lift his head above the water level. Jim dragged himself over, lifting Clayton clear of the water so he could breathe.

"Unhook your foot," Jim hissed in his ear, "I can't hold you up for much longer."

Clayton tried to comply, the explosive jolt of agony racing down his leg from his shattered ankle causing him to lurch back, his head again slipping below the surface for a second before Jim pushed him clear. "I can't, it hurts too bad. Man, you wouldn't believe how much it hurts. I think it's broken."

"Hang on, let me take a look," Jim said.

Holding Clayton up with one hand out of the water, Jim shifted position and could immediately see the problem. As Clayton had fallen, the wheel had shifted, threading Clayton's leg over and under the wheel, and pinning it against the dashboard. Clayton was right. From the unnatural angle in which it was hanging, it was most definitely broken.

"How's it looking?" Clayton said, panic seeping into his voice.

"It's not too bad," Jim said, hoping the lie would go undetected.

"It really hurts, man," Clayton moaned.

Jim shifted position, his arms tiring from holding his friend out of the water. "Don't worry, Tom and Fernando will be here to help us soon enough," Jim replied, wondering what the hell was taking so long.

Outside, Tom and Fernando were trying to climb up the outer structure of the truck to no avail. Neither of them was particularly strong swimmers, and the thrashing and jerking of the truck as it was pulled ever deeper, had put off those who had initially joined the rescue attempt, leaving Tom and his brother alone in the rescue efforts.

The trailer groaned as the creature pulled against it, shearing loose one of the four housings holding its harness in place and dragging the trailer even deeper so that two thirds of it was now submerged. Back in the cab, the movement of the truck shattered the window that was submerged, flooding the cab with a rush of seawater. Both Jim and Clayton were instantly submerged. The truck rocked, and for a moment, looked as if it were going to tip onto its roof, yet, somehow it remained upright.

Clayton thrashed under water, the agony in his leg second to the desperation to grasp a breath of air. For the second time, Jim pushed his head out of the water to relative safety, although now, his face was barely above the waterline and the position of his body meant he could go no further. He looked Jim in the eye. Neither had to say anything. They knew if the truck were pulled any deeper, Clayton would die.

A shadow moved overhead. Jim and Clayton saw Tom looking down into the cab from the passenger side door. "Hang on, I'm coming down," he said as he started to climb through the open window.

"No," Jim said, "he's stuck. You need to cut the whale loose. If it pulls us any deeper, he's done for."

"We can get you out."

"Look at his fuckin' foot, man," Jim screamed.

Tom did, and saw the way it was twisted around the steering wheel. Fernando had joined him at the window. "Alright," Tom said, "we'll be as quick as we can."

With that he was gone, his brother in tow.

"Don't leave me here, man," Clayton stuttered as the water lapped against his face. "Don't you dare. I know what you did. I'll tell them. I'll tell them you killed that man."

Jim knew it was the fear talking, and yet at the same time, Clayton was right. He looked around the confines of their prison, the water filled cab, which was eerily silent. It dawned on him that nobody apart from Clayton knew it was he who had shot the driver of the truck. They were both wearing balaclavas. Like a snowball rolling down a hill, one idea grew into another, then another.

How easy would it be? He asked himself. *How easy just to release his grip on Claytons head and shoulders and let it fall beneath the waves? How much effort would it take to hold him down as he thrashed in his desperation for air? How long can an average person hold his breath for underwater? One minute? Two?*

He locked eyes with Clayton, and there was an unspoken knowledge of what was about to happen.

"Wait, don't-"

It was all Clayton could manage before Jim pushed his head under the water.

Outside, Tom and Fernando were making their way down the side of the truck, stepping carefully on the steel side rails towards the rear. Between the gaps, they could see the huge hulking shape of the creature as it thrashed against its confines. They could also see the bodies of those who were riding with it in the back, floating on the surface, arms bobbing with the tide.

"Jesus, this wasn't meant to happen this way," Fernando said, voice trembling as he followed his brother.

Tom didn't answer. He was more concerned with what was below him. He could see the creature partly free of its harness, and was horrified by what he saw.

Fernando started to climb down over the edge when Tom grabbed him.

"Wait."

"We don't have time," Fernando replied. "We have to move fast."

"You can't go in there."

"Why not?"

"Because that's not a whale."

"Don't be ridiculous."

"Just look at it, Fred."

Fernando followed his brother's gaze to the gaps between the metal side rails. It was plain enough to see. The creature had almost entirely slipped free of its harness, exposing its grey green body and array of tree trunk like tentacles.

"What the hell-"

Fernando was cut off as the creature lurched again, dragging the trailer deeper and knocking Tom and Jim off balance. Tom fell into the sea, Fernando's leg slipped between the rails, his foot making contact with the creature. He could only watch as its harness finally gave way. The creature was free of its restraints.

Tom resurfaced, coughing up seawater. He grasped the rear axle of the truck, hooking an elbow around the greasy shaft. He watched in awe as the creature freed itself. It lingered for a moment in the water, mere feet from Tom, then with a flick of its flippers, was moving into deeper waters, the wake it left behind rocking the trailer.

"What the hell *was* that," Fernando said, staring after the creature.

"I don't know, just help me up," Tom grunted.

Fernando pulled his brother back up onto the rail of the truck, and the pair hurried back towards the cab. As they arrived, Jim climbed out, eyes wide and lip trembling.

"I couldn't help him, I tried but I couldn't keep his head up."

Tom and Fernando looked into the cab at Clayton's body as it bobbed under the water, submerged from head to chest.

"Holy shit, this is bad, this is really bad," Fernando mumbled.

"It was an accident. We need to wait for the police," Tom countered.

"No man, we *can't*," Jim cut in. "He lost it, he had a gun. He shot the driver..."

"Not Clayton, no way," Fernando said, looking down at the floating corpse of his friend.

"I saw it! I was right there!" Jim screamed.

"Where the hell did he get a gun?"

"How the fuck should I know? All I can tell you is he had one, and shot a guy with it."

"Holy shit," Fernando said, then turned to his brother, "what do we do now?"

"Let's get out of here. We need to lay low and figure this out," Tom said.

"Where the hell are we supposed to go?"

"Anywhere, just away from here before the police arrive."

"What about Clayton?" Fernando said.

The three of them looked down into the cab.

"We can't do anything for him now. Come on, let's get the hell out of here," Tom replied.

CHAPTER NINE

Forty minutes after the truck had first slewed into the ocean, Andrews strode towards the barricaded section of beach, pushing past the crowd that had gathered in huge numbers to gawp at the spectacle. He flashed his ID at the guard on at the barrier and was granted access. Gus Freeman waddled towards him, wiping sweat from his brow.

"What the hell happened here, Gus?"

"Bunch of animal rights nuts hijacked the truck and drove it into the water."

"Fuck. Greenpeace?" Andrews snapped as they walked away from the eavesdropping crowd.

"Not this time. Bunch of teenagers by the looks of things. Driver drowned in the cab. The others managed to get away. We're taking statements from witnesses, but everyone was so preoccupied with what was happening, it's not much use trying to get any description."

"I thought the driver was shot?" Andrews said as they strode towards the surf.

"He was. I meant the guy who took over the vehicle."

"Any ID on him?"

"Drivers licence in his wallet. Clayton Sanders, just turned seventeen."

"Family?" Andrews asked.

"We're trying to get them. Parents are divorced. His mother lives in Portland. We're trying to get the father at his office."

"Did anyone see anything?"

"No," Freeman said, wiping his forearm against his head. He was struggling to keep pace with Andrews, almost having to run to match his stride. "In a way, it was lucky the trailer went over on its side. Blocked the, uh, cargo from view. People are assuming it was a whale."

"That's one positive at least. Goddamnit, Gus, this is the last thing I needed. Please tell me the tracker is still implanted into the creature."

"Uh, I'm not sure, sir. As far as I know it is."

"Jesus Christ, what the hell are we going to do?" Andrews said, staring at the overturned truck and the army of government officials in black wetsuits, which were swarming all over it. Up above, news helicopters hovered like angry flies.

"How many were involved?"

"Not exactly sure, sir," Freeman stammered. "Witnesses say there was either one or two in the truck and another two or three clearing the way for it to get onto the beach. As I said, most of them were preoccupied with gawping at the scene."

"In other words, we don't know?"

"Unfortunately, that seems to be the case," Freeman muttered.

"I want them found."

"We can deploy local law enforcement, sir, they will-"

"No," Andrews interjected, "no police. We can't risk this getting out into the public, not yet anyway."

"What should we do, sir?"

"Go round the witnesses again, see if anyone has video of it. Every man and his dog have a camera phone these days. Surely to God, someone got a video or a photograph of these people."

"Yes sir," Freeman said, then cleared this throat. "Uh, sir, Commander Tomlinson has called twice for you, now demanding you get in contact with him."

"I will, just as soon as I have something to tell him," Andrews snapped. "First off, I want this scene cleared up. Last thing we want is a crowd of people speculating as to what's happened. Leak the story that it was a blue whale transfer that was intercepted by animal rights activists. Put the dead kid's picture on the news. Make sure he's linked to killing the driver of the truck, and ask   anyone who knows him to get in contact. Someone, somewhere, will crawl out of the woodwork, and for the love of God, get those damn news choppers out of the air."

"And what about the, uh, other problem," Freeman said, nodding towards the open water.

"Leave that with me. Do you have a phone on you? I left mine at the aquarium."

Freeman handed Andrews his phone.

"Thanks," Andrews said as he decided it was better to deal with

Tomlinson sooner rather than later.

He punched in the commander's number, surprised when rather than his secretary, Tomlinson himself answered on the second ring.

"You better have good news for me, Andrews," the commander snapped.

"Actually, I don't. I have control of the situation here, but unfortunately, our cargo is missing."

"Are you telling me our multi-million dollar mission has been derailed by a bunch of kids?" Tomlinson screamed.

"Please, calm down, sir, it's under-"

"Don't you tell me to calm down. Have you any idea how serious this is?"

"All due respect, sir, I do. I was there the first time, up close and personal with this things mother in Antarctica," Andrews snapped.

"Well then, you know what's at stake. Out at sea this thing can grow to adulthood. The last thing we need is another three hundred foot fucking problem swimming around in our oceans."

"I'll track it down. You have my word."

"You know, I wouldn't be at all surprised if it was Rainwater and Thompson who were responsible for this."

"Doubtful, sir, they have little contact anymore. They've moved on."

"That's an assumption at best. Bring them in. Question them."

"Sir, wouldn't our resources be better used in finding the creature?"

"For someone who has spent the last five years misappropriating government funds, you are in *no* position to talk about resources. Bring them in and do it now. Then get out there and kill this fish."

"Kill it, sir? Don't you mean capture it?"

"No, I want it killed. Project Blue is officially terminated."

"But, sir-"

"Don't say another word, Andrews. You're clinging onto your job by the skin of your teeth. Think very carefully before you speak again."

Andrews pushed his anger aside and took a deep breath. "Yes sir. I'll get right to work."

"You better. This project has been one screw up after the other.

Fix it, do it now and you might just save your job."

The line clicked off in Andrews's ear. He handed the phone back to Freeman and walked to the water's edge, staring out to sea. For the first time in five years, he felt genuine fear gnawing at his gut.

CHAPTER TEN

Thought at one time to be a creature of myth and legend, the forty three foot colossal squid moved north, planning to feed on the edge of the Antarctic Ocean waters, which were its natural habitat. The squid propelled itself deeper, using its arrow shaped tail to dive to three thousand feet in its quest for food. Armed with suckers on its tentacles, which were ringed with tiny teeth, the colossal squid was also equipped with sharp barbed hooks on its limbs, which made it a ferocious predator.

A half mile away, the near hundred foot long creature circled, weighing up its potential prey. Conditioned by a life of routine and regular feeding times, the creature was struggling to adapt to its newfound freedom. Its senses were inundated with information sent to it by the abundance of life within the oceans. It had already feasted on a giant sea turtle, and was now eager to feed again. Sensing the squid's depth adjustment, the creature followed suit, delving deeper into the icy waters and keeping a respectful distance. Due to the network of nerves running over and under the creature's snout, it was able to read the ocean, detecting the electrical impulse of its potential prey from miles away. The sheer darkness of the deep waters was nothing but a minor inconvenience for the creature, as it halved the distance between itself and the slow moving squid.

Powerless to outrun its pursuer, the squid was left with no option but to face its attacker head on. In addition to its barbed appendages, the squid was equipped with a razor sharp beak, which was an impressive eleven inches in length and enough to make most predators think twice. However, it had never encountered anything like this particular type of creature, whose own set of forty eight, fifteen inch, backward facing serrated teeth were more than a match for any defence the squid would be able to muster.

The creature flicked its massive fluke, tentacles at its side to achieve maximum efficiency as it powered through the water. The squid, realising it was hopelessly outmatched, started to dive, hoping that by descending to colder waters, its attacker would give up the chase. Undaunted and driven by its lust to feed, the creature followed, its genetic makeup meaning that although cold, the waters in which the squid dived were nowhere even close to the usual Antarctic waters, which made up the creatures natural habitat.

Closing to within eight feet of the fleeing squid, the creature burst forward, ten foot wide jaws clamping onto the squid and tearing it in half. The creature quivered as it devoured the lower half of the squid, automatically reaching out with its tentacles to grab at the front half of the creature that was starting to sink towards the bottom. Finishing its meal, the creature pulled the upper half towards it gaping maw, quickly devouring the remains. Hovering for a moment in five thousand feet of water, the creature picked up on another signal, a series of vibrations, which instinct told it meant a creature in distress. With a flick of its giant fluke, it was on the move, looking for another opportunity to satisfy its perpetual hunger.

II

The motel was a seedy, grimy place where questions weren't asked about the nature of the stay, as long as money was paid up front. The walls were paper thin and the decor grubby, but it was private. Jim, Fernando and Tom sat in the room, perched on the edge of the two double beds and watching the television coverage of their antics. Marie was sitting against the wall, knees pulled up to her chin and not speaking to anyone. She had been the same ever since they fled the beach. The others watched the coverage as it showed footage of the truck driver's body by the roadside, covered by a sheet as the report stated the gunman had been found dead on the scene at the beach.

"This is fucked up, man," Tom said, his voice wavering. "They're going to find us."

"Nobody knows who we are, just relax." Jim said, surprised how calm he felt considering everything that had happened.

"Why the hell would he do this? Where the fuck did he get the gun from?" Tom replied, standing and pacing the room.

"You need to calm down, man," Jim said. "As for the gun, I didn't know he had it till he shot the guy."

"And you didn't think to stop him?"

"Hey, what could I do? He wouldn't listen. No way am I taking on someone who just shot a guy."

"It's not Jim's fault," Fernando said to his brother. "We need to stick together. I think we can all agree this is all fucked up."

"This is gonna end bad for us. Don't you get it?" Tom said. "It won't take them long to ID Clayton. From there, how long do you think it's gonna take for them to find out who his friends were? We can't hide from this."

Although he didn't show it outwardly, a surge of panic raced through Jim. He wondered if it were true, if the police could find them so quickly, and if so, could they prove it was he who was guilty and not Clayton. For the first time, it dawned on him that he was responsible for the deaths of two people.

"You okay?" Fernando said, snapping Jim back to the present.

"Yeah, I'm fine. Still in shock I think," he mumbled, turning back towards the television.

Tom sat next to his brother, elbows on knees, head hanging low. "What the hell are we going to do?" he whispered.

Fernando was spared from having to answer by the knock at the door. Jim and Fernando shot worried glances to each other as Tom stood.

"Relax, it's just Joanne. I asked her to bring us some stuff."

Tom opened the door and let his girlfriend in. She handed over a rucksack.

"There's the stuff you asked for. Change of clothes and some money," she said as she closed the door. "What the hell happened? I couldn't get away from the aquarium. They locked the place down tight after word got out of what you'd done."

"It all went wrong, Clayton had a gun, and he shot the driver of the truck."

"Clayton? That can't be," Joanne said, looking straight at Jim.

My God, she knows.

"That's what happened," Jim said. "Maybe we didn't know him as well as we thought."

"How did he die?" she asked, still staring at Jim.

"Well, they were trapped in the cab and-"

"I was asking Jim," Joanne said, cutting Fernando off.

Jim shifted position, looking anywhere but at Joanne. "Well, it's like he said. We were stuck in the cab. He tried to climb out to get help and got his foot caught in the wheel. I held him up out of the water for as long as I could, but that thing in the back kept moving and pulling the trailer deeper. He drowned. There was nothing I could do."

"It's true," Tom said, putting an arm around Joanne, "Fernando and me saw it, his foot was all mangled and twisted."

"It all seems a little too easy."

"Look, go easy on him. We've all had a big shock. Obviously, this has gotten out of hand. We need to decide what to do," Tom said, pacing the room from flimsy door to dirty bathroom and back.

"You're running aren't you? That's why you asked for the money," Joanne said.

"It's an option. There's a lot to be said for turning ourselves in. After all, we didn't actually do anything wrong," Tom replied as he sat on the edge of the bed.

"We did a lot wrong," Fernando mumbled, "just look at the TV screen."

They looked at the images of police and officials swarming all over the beach scene.

"Jesus," Joanne mumbled, "this is crazy."

"We can't give ourselves up," Jim blurted. He cleared his throat and went on. "What I mean is that they'll pin this on us as accessories."

"You sound like you have something to hide," Joanne said.

"No, not at all. I just think we should lay low for a while and see how things develop."

"Convenient."

"If you have a problem with me, then just spit it out," Jim snapped.

"Hey, everyone just calm down," Fernando said. "There's something else you need to know."

"Not now," Tom said, looking at his brother.

"They need to know."

"Not now, we can talk about it later."

"What is it?" Joanne said, looking from Fernando to Tom. "What are you both hiding?"

Fernando looked at his brother, and then shifted his gaze to Joanne. "Whatever we set free from that trailer, it wasn't a whale."

"Enough of the monster stories!" Marie screamed. They all looked at her, tears streaming down her cheeks. "This is how this whole thing started, just shut up about it!"

"It's not a story," Tom said, "it's true."

"What do you mean?" Joanne asked.

"We were right there at the back. We were going to cut it loose before it dragged the trailer any deeper. Whatever it was, it was no whale."

"What did you see?"

"Not much. It was covered mostly and in its harness. Its body was like a greenish colour and it had tentacles."

"But it was huge," Jim said, "and heavy. No squid can grow that big can it?"

"No, it can't," Tom replied. "The more I think about it, the surer I am that we've made a massive mistake in whatever it was."

"But what *was* it, Tom. You saw it, you must have *some* idea, "Joanne said.

"I don't know what it was. All I know is that it's something I've never seen before."

Joanne looked at Tom, the troubled look in his eye unfamiliar to her. "Are you sayin' those stories about something being held in there for the last five years could be true?"

"Yeah, I think so, and whatever it is, we just let it loose."

They were silent for a while, the only sound in the room coming from the television as the news recycled the same report from the beach. Jim stood and strode towards the door.

"Where the hell are you going?" Fernando said.

"I need a drink."

"You can't just go out there now. Not with this-"

"What?" Jim said to Fernando. "Nobody has anything on us. Hell, for all we know, nobody is even looking for us."

"That's wishful thinking," Fernando muttered.

"Yeah," Joanne said, "who knows if you will even come back if you leave now."

"What the hell is that supposed to mean?" Jim hissed.

"You know what I mean. Everyone knows your history. Trouble with the police, a history of causing problems. I just don't want you running out and leaving everyone else to get the blame."

"You really think I'd do that?" Jim grunted.

"If the cap fits," she fired back.

"Fuck you."

"Hey, don't talk to her like that," Tom said, taking a step towards Jim.

"Sorry, man, but she's been niggling at me since she walked through the door. Say what you want, but if things are about to change and we have to spend the next couple of weeks hiding out, then I wanna enjoy this last little bit of freedom. The rest of you are welcome to stay here if you want to and watch this same old shit on the news, but I won't do it. I'm gonna go find a bar and have a few drinks and toast my friend."

Nobody spoke as he walked past them and opened the door. One by one, they followed, deciding that maybe, just maybe, he was right.

CHAPTER ELEVEN

Immediately following the incident at Cocoa Beach, a message was sent to the C.I.A and Homeland Security to compile a list of potential people or groups who may be responsible for carrying out such a daring attack. Top of the list, above the usual animal rights activists, were the names Henry Rainwater and Clara Thompson. Within an hour of the news breaking, both had been rounded up and transported by Helicopter to the Pentagon. Deliberately kept apart from each other, they were placed into separate holding cells for questioning. Such was the importance of finding out quickly who was responsible, Tomlinson himself was on site, and insisted on being involved with the questioning. Andrews had flown in too, despite having a mammoth workload already. Tomlinson had insisted he be on site to speak to them as he had a personal relationship with both parties.

He walked the wide corridor towards where they were being held in separate rooms. He knew Tomlinson was in with Clara, and so he was left with Rainwater. He opened the door to the office where he was waiting, shocked at just how much his physical appearance had changed. When Andrews had last seen him five years earlier, he was a slim, steely eyed fisherman. Now he was a bearded, overweight, and world weary excuse for a man. Even before he could take his seat, Andrews could smell the booze seeping out of his pores. Andrews took his seat and looked Rainwater in the eye, trying to see anything of the man he once knew.

"Do you know why we brought you here?" he asked.

"I can guess. I just hope I'm wrong," Rainwater grunted.

"Have you been drinking?"

"So what if I have? Can't a man have a drink when he wants to?"

"Looks like more than just one," Andrews countered.

"So whaddya want?"

Andrews cleared his throat. "Well, as you know, this morning there was an incident on Cocoa Beach. I assume you've seen the news."

"I don't have a TV. Even so, before you go any further, forget it."

"Forget what?" Andrews said, genuinely confused.

"You know. I told you everything I knew about what happened in the ice cave. I also promised not to speak a word of it to anyone, which I haven't. Whatever reason you brought me in here, I didn't do it."

"Look, Henry, I assumed you would know why you're here, but the fact that you don't makes this more difficult." Andrews waited for a response, and was met only by a glassy stare. "There's no easy way to say this, so I'll just come out and say it. Back when we collapsed the ross ice shelf-"

"You didn't collapse shit. It was my friend, my best friend who did that and you and your government didn't even acknowledge it," Rainwater slurred.

"You know the reasons for that, but frankly it's beside the point."

"No matter what your reasons, that man died a hero. Those bastard things deserved to die."

"We captured one."

For the first time, Rainwater appeared to be paying attention. The glaze lifted from his eyes and he sat up straight in his seat. "What do you mean?"

"It wasn't intentional. One of the juveniles escaped the ice cave before it collapsed. It swam straight into our holding tank on the battleship we had prepared for the adult."

"You better be joking, Andrews."

"No, I'm not. We moved the creature to a secured facility in Florida where it's been under observation ever since. That was, until this morning. We were transporting the creature to a new location when the truck was hijacked. Long story short, the creature was set free and we want you to help us get it back."

"You're telling me there is another one of those things out there in the ocean?"

Andrews loosened his tie, squirming under the fierce gaze of Rainwater. "Yes, I'm afraid so."

He expected Rainwater to scream or perhaps even launch

himself across the desk. Instead, he leaned in, speaking in a near whisper, the alcohol on his breath hot and pungent. "You know what we went through to kill that thing. *All* of us. You know the sacrifices we made."

"I know, please-"

"My friend died to make sure that thing was stopped. *You* agreed it had to happen. You were there."

"Henry, please-"

"And now you drag me in here to tell me you've had one in captivity for all this time, and now that it's escaped you want *my* help to find it."

"Just let me explain. I-"

"Shut up," Rainwater hissed. "Let me make it crystal clear for you. This isn't my problem anymore. Whatever it is you want, I'm not interested. This fucking monster has already taken too much from me. It's left me a shell. My friend died, my brother's widow couldn't take anymore and killed herself. Don't you think I've sacrificed enough?"

"Please, calm down. Let me explain what we need-"

"No. I don't want to know. This is your monster now. You clean up the mess."

"Henry, listen to reason. You know how dangerous this creature is. If we don't capture it before it reaches its full size, then-"

"Save it. I'm not interested. You might be better speaking to Clara. She's a money grabbing attention seeking bitch these days by all accounts. I'm sure she'd help you if you waved a handful of money at her."

"Please, Henry, you have a responsibility-"

"No, I don't. My responsibility ended when that ice cave came down. If you chose to capture this thing and then let it go again, then it's your responsibility. I don't have the strength to go through this again."

"Can you live with yourself if this thing starts to kill again?" Andrews asked.

"I struggle to live with myself every day as it is. You think I didn't see it on your face when you walked in here? Fucking look at me. This is what your creature did to me. Nothing good can come from this. Only pain and death. You should have left it to die with its mother."

"Henry, please, you're making a huge mistake."

"No, *you're* the one who made the mistake. This time you can deal with it yourself. You're no better than Russo."

"That's below the belt," Andrews said. "You must understand there's a chain of command. I have orders too, it's how it works."

"I don't care about that. I just want out of here."

"What is there for you out there? What kind of life are you going back to? How long will getting shitfaced drunk everyday satisfy you? This is a chance to redeem yourself, it-"

"You may as well just stop. Yes I drink, but only to blot out the pain of what happened last time. Sometimes it works, sometimes it doesn't, but I'll tell you this, it's better than the thought of going out after that thing again. Not after what happened last time."

"Is there nothing I can say to change your mind?" Andrews said.

"This fish could eat its way around every coastline from here to Australia, and you still couldn't get me to go out there. Get some other idiot to do your dirty work. You're wasting your time asking me."

Andrews nodded. Far from being surprised, he could actually see Rainwaters point for the most part. The man had already suffered enough, and by the condition he was in, there was no way he had anything to do with the creature escaping.

"Oaky, Henry," he said with a sigh, "point taken. If you wait here I'll have someone escort you off the premises."

"You have to kill this thing. You must know capturing it isn't an option."

It was the most lucid thing Rainwater had said since he arrived. For a split second, Andrews saw beyond the fog induced by alcohol to the man who Rainwater used to be.

"Well, that won't be your concern. Soon enough, you'll be back to your life of drinking and self-pity."

"Forget the guilt trip. This is your mess. Not mine."

"And I'll clean it up."

"By killing it?"

"As I said, that's not your concern."

"You surely know that trying to capture this thing is a mistake?

Remember what happened last time. Really think about it."

"I remember, and trust me, I won't make the same mistakes again."

CHAPTER TWELVE

Greg Michaels threw another shot of Vodka down his neck, the fire barely bothering him anymore. Perched on the end seat of the bar in his usual spot, he rapped his knuckles on the oak surface. Like magic, the bartender appeared, refilling his glass, knowing by now not to make small talk. The leather skinned Australian pushed his fringe out of his eyes and thought it was a wonder how easily he had adapted to doing things left handed. The fleshy stump of his right hand brought back memories - memories of the time when everything went to hell. Many things were hazy in his day to day life, which seemed to muddle from one day to the next, a monotonous groundhog day of misery and frustration. The memories of *that* day though, would never die. He closed his eyes and it came to him in all too horrific clarity - the day, which had started out as an easy charter to take a tourist shark spotting and ended in disaster.

It had all gone fine until he and his paying customer was down in the cage and some...*thing* came out of the darkness, which changed the trajectory of his life forever. Something so immense it defied logic. He took another sip from his glass, savouring both flavour and memories alike.

The creature propelled itself forward. Greg watched in awe as its greenish grey body passed him, and so large was the creature, it filled his field of vision for what felt like an age. He saw a sliver of sharp teeth in the partially open jaw, as the vast animal snagged the side of beef away with a single, effortless bite. He knew he should check on his client, but was so mesmerised by the giant yards away from him, he couldn't bring himself to tear his eyes away from it. The creature nudged the cage as it passed, and for a split second, Greg lost his grip, snatching twice at the bars before managing to restore his hold. It was then he saw the great white ascend from below. It was big, at least an eighteen footer. Even it looked tiny in comparison to the immense creature. The white had been drawn in

85

by the bloody carcass, and unlike its brethren, it had not fled from the creature. It was only when Greg saw the other sharks appearing out of the darkness that he thought he understood what was happening. Hunters in their own right, the sharks were ready to respond to the new threat by challenging its supremacy.

It was at that precise second that fear replaced the thrill, and Greg turned towards his client, who was still staring wide eyed at the creature. It seemed he hadn't noticed the sharks, which Greg thought could be a good thing. He shook Paul by the shoulder, snapping him to attention. His intention had been to give the instruction to ascend, yet, when he looked towards the surface, the path was blocked by great whites, which were circling and waiting to attack. As experienced as he was, he would never risk swimming to the surface, especially as the whites looked ready to attack at any given moment. Instead, he pointed to the cage, swimming to the roof and pulling open the hatch. Paul had noticed the sharks now too, and his eyes flicked wildly between the giant creature and its potential attackers. Greg banged on the cage to get Paul's attention, watching as one of the whites cautiously darted closer to the creature, then retreated. He banged his fist on the cage roof again, and although Paul briefly looked at him, he didn't move. He released his grip on the door and moved towards the edge of the cage roof, grabbing Paul by the shoulder and finally getting his attention. Perhaps it was the fear or desperation in his eyes, or the gravity of the situation finally hitting home which forced him into action. He inched his way up the side of the cage between frightened glances at the gathering sharks. Greg dragged him the rest of the way, yanked open the hatch and shoved Paul inside. He followed and pulled the door closed, and not a moment too soon. One of the larger whites, a twenty two foot male, charged towards the creature and snapped at one of its tentacles. The reaction was devastating. The creature lunged for the shark, shearing away a huge flap of its underbelly in a single bite. As the great white convulsed and sank into the depths, its brethren as one began to attack.

Greg picked up his vodka shot with a shaking hand and finished it in one, hoping it would hurry and blot out the rest. It never worked though. It never stopped it replaying in his mind. Once again, he knocked on the bar and waited until his glass was filled. The shark attack was terrifying enough, but even that didn't compare to what came next. The creature had fought them off easily, decimating them as if they were no more than a minor annoyance. One of the sharks the creature had attacked - an eighteen foot male - had slewed away from the creature, its underbelly sheared away, blood and entrails churning into the ocean, and had come to rest on the cage roof, pinning the hatch closed and showering Greg and his customer with hot blood and innards. As terrifying as it was, it paled in comparison to the sight of the creature as it came towards the cage to finish off its meal. That was when he knew they would have to escape, and as the creature approached, Greg swam to the top of the cage, desperately trying to open the hatch and get to freedom. Even now, years after the fact, he liked to convince himself he was looking to help his customer too, yet he knew deep down it was his own self-preservation which was key. Something had happened then. Some kind of immense explosion under the surface, which sealed the fate of both him and Mr Milla, and shaped the future in which he was now a prisoner.

Greg had managed to force enough of the hatch open against the dead weight of the shark's corpse when the concussion wave hit. The shockwave rocked the cage violently, snapping his hand – which was trapped between cage and hatch- like kindling. With no protection from the blast, Paul was slammed against inner wall of the cage, his head smashing against the bars as he was flung like a ragdoll. With his mangled hand trapped in the hatch and the full weight of the shark's body pinning it down, Greg hung helplessly, trying to shake away the ringing in his ears as he peered through his cracked facemask. Something caught his eye. He looked around as multiple species of dead fish began to float to the surface. All sizes, all varieties. He saw a dolphin, floating vertically past the cage rotating in a graceful arc as it climbed. The ocean had gone from battleground to a macabre showcase of the dead, as species after species floated to the surface.

He had heard about this before. Some people used to fish this way back before it was made illegal. Blast fishing where dynamite would be tossed into the water would cause the stunned fish's swim

RETURN TO THE DEEP

bladders to rupture, resulting in a horrible, painful death. Although he could see a huge number of animals floating to the surface, he knew it could have been worse, as many of the larger species of fish had already fled away from the carnage that had taken place. He shifted position where he hung by his arm, biting down hard on his regulator as pain jolted from his wrist. It was then that he saw the creature. It too was motionless and gently floating belly up towards the surface, its tentacles splayed out and drifting in the current. Again, he was mesmerised by the sheer scale of the animal. It was completely unlike anything else he had ever seen before, and fears aside, he appreciated its majesty.

In the cage, Greg struggled to free himself. His ears were still ringing from the explosion, and salt water dripped into his eyes from the hairline crack in his facemask, but he was otherwise in reasonable shape. He stopped flailing and checked the gauge on his trapped right hand, confirming his fears. The small wristwatch like device told him the air tank on his back was running dangerously close to empty. He estimated he had less than fifteen minutes of air left before he would drown. The thought of death renewed his energy, and he redoubled his efforts, alternating between trying to yank his arm free and getting enough leverage to displace the shark corpse, neither of which seemed to be doing anything but sending explosive jolts of paint through his broken wrist. He began to suck air greedily from the regulator, knowing every breath was precious but still unable to help himself. On the floor of the cage, Paul didn't stir, and had slumped to the side, a steady cloud of blood mushrooming from the wound in the back of his head. Faced with the fact he was never going to be able to move the dead shark that was pinning the lid of the cage closed, Greg knew he would have to make a drastic choice. The floor of the cage was also hinged in case of emergency, and he knew it was his one and only way out. First, he had to free himself. He looked at his mangled hand, and realised what he needed to do.

How much do you want to live?

He asked himself as he twisted and tugged at his arm.

How far will you go to survive?

It was then that absolute clarity came to him and he stopped struggling. It was extreme, and he knew he would have to do it

88

quickly before his air supply ran out. Despite the urgency, there were a lot of questions he didn't have the answer to.

Could he go through with it?

Could he withstand the pain, and if he did, could he get to a doctor in time?

What if he passed out halfway through?

Answers or no answers, it didn't matter. There was no other choice. Taking a deep breath of precious air, he unsheathed the hunting knife from his diving belt, the blade warping the light as he held it to his face. It was a good knife. Sharp too. He hoped it wouldn't hurt, maybe if enough numbness had set in...

No.

Enough delays. He had a job to do, and every second was precious.

Pleasedonthurtpleasedonthurtpleasedonthurt

He repeated it over and over in his head, praying he would have the strength to do what needed to be done. As he began to hack through the soft flesh of his wrist, prying bone away from bone, shearing tendon and flesh, brilliant, white hot agony surged through his body, and he bit on the regulator hard enough to fracture two teeth. As he carved away at his wrist through a cloud of blood, tears streaming down his face and mingling with the salt water that had already penetrated the mask, another question came to him.

What happens if the creature wakes up?

He looked down at his stump, resting it on the bar.

Yes.

There are certain extremes a man will go to in order to survive. Extremes that to some might be beyond their ability to complete or even comprehend. The question was always the same, and a simple one at that. The question was: How much did a person want to live? At that time, Greg wanted to live more than anything else in the world, which made the next decision frighteningly simple. Even so, the pain was unreal. Unlike anything else he had ever experienced or would ever be able to express to anyone who might ask him how it felt. Although he could never explain it, he could remember it more than well enough. Like the rest, it was still fresh in his mind.

Somehow, he hadn't passed out. Maybe it was the adrenaline or the desire to survive. Whatever the reason, Greg was still conscious. It had been close. The soft tissues weren't too bad, but the nerves felt charged with millions of vaults of electricity, as he had sliced through them. Even so, he was still woozy. The knife grinding against bone as he separated his wrist had sounded incredibly loud in his head, and he had to count backwards from ten to keep conscious. Knife blade trembling, he cut through the last of the gristle and was at last free, sinking to the bottom of the cage and leaving a mushrooming cloud of blood behind as if he were some kind of bizarre distress flare. The relief lasted only for seconds until the pain found him, bringing his nerve endings alive with fierce agony. He clutched his bleeding stump to his chest, and sank towards the bottom of the cage.

Fortunately, he had been able to open the secondary hatch in the cage floor and escape, swimming to the surface and coaxing his customer's wife to help activate the controls and pull the winch to the surface. There was no sign of the creature which had attacked them, and even though they managed to get the cage up, dislodge the dead shark and free Mr Milla, he died before help could arrive, the force of the explosion slamming him against the cage and splitting his skull like a ripe melon. One thing that had eluded Greg almost daily since it happened is why he hadn't gone for the floor hatch from the start. He supposed it was pointless to worry too much about it, and suspected under the unique circumstances, he could be forgiven. However, that didn't change things for his recently deceased customer, or the grieving widow he left behind.

Later, Mrs Milla would file charges against him for gross negligence. Advised to settle out of court for way more than he could afford, he had paid her off and lost his business in the process. Nobody of course believed him about the creature. Why would they? Even so, that beast had managed in just a few moments to destroy his life totally. Now, he had become a bitter recluse, living out his days scraping by on what little disability money he received from the government, and drifting through life with an ever burning anger and frustration towards the creature and the mess it had made of his life.

It was because of this he had been listening in to the conversation on the table behind him. He had taken a good look at the group when he had passed them on his way to the bathroom. Three men and two women, late teens to early twenties at a guess. They had been speaking in hushed tones about the Cocoa Beach incident, and Greg was more certain they were involved with every passing moment. More interesting was their description as they spoke of what was in the trailer.

It sounded for all the world like the same creature (although on a smaller scale) which had destroyed his life. Draining his glass, he watched as the bartender approached to refill it. Greg shook his head.

He wanted to stay sober enough to hear what else they had to say. Already, he was starting to formulate an idea.

CHAPTER THIRTEEN

It was the morning after the night before. After being transported by Helicopter from The Pentagon back to his apartment in Portland, Rainwater had spent the rest of the night much like every other - getting absolutely shitfaced on whatever drink he could lay his hands on. It took a few moments to realise that the steady thumping he could hear wasn't just the onset of a hangover, but someone pounding on his door. He was pretty sure he'd paid his rent, and couldn't think of anyone else he owed money to. He considered ignoring the door until they went away, and yet, every crash of fist against wood only further aggravated his headache.

"Alrightimcoming," he slurred as he rolled out of bed, sending the empty bottle of scotch rolling across the hardwood floor as he stumbled past it.

Pulling on a pair of jeans, which barely fastened anymore due to his ever expanding waistline, he staggered to the door, intending to give whoever was on the other side of it a piece of his mind for waking him so early. He yanked the door open.

"What?" he grunted.

Clara stood on the other side of the door; not doing anywhere nearly as good a job as Andrews about hiding her shock at his appearance. "Can I come in?" She said.

"I didn't expect to see you here," Rainwater said, scratching at his thick, matted hair. "It's a bit early for visitors."

"It's almost four in the afternoon," she said, frowning. "Jesus, you look like shit."

"Thanks," Rainwater muttered, still leaning across the doorframe.

"So...can I come in or not?"

"Whatever," he said, opening the door to allow her access.

She wrinkled her nose as she looked around the room, which was littered with empty bottles, dirty washing and empty plastic ready meal trays for one.

"When was the last time you opened a damn window in here?" she said as she strode across the room, yanking open the curtains.

"I like my privacy," he muttered as he sat on the edge of the bed to roll a cigarette.

Clara opened the window as far as it would go then turned to Rainwater.

"Sit down over there if you like," he said, pointing to the armchair that was piled high with clothes. "Just throw those on the floor."

"I'm fine."

"Alright, then what *do* you want?" He said, angry at how good she looked, and for the first time ashamed of his own appearance.

"You know why I'm here. It's about last night."

"Andrews?" Rainwater said as he lit his cigarette, enjoying the first hit of nicotine of the day.

"Yeah. He told me all about what had happened. About the creature."

"I hope you told him to go fuck himself. That's what I did."

"Actually, I didn't. That's why I'm here."

"What do you mean?"

"I mean I accepted his offer. I'm leading the team to hunt it down."

"You can't do that," Henry said, standing and taking a step towards her. Clara took a compensatory step back, face twisting in disgust.

"I can do what I want. You don't control me," she hissed.

"I'm not trying to control you, but you know what we went through before. What Mackay went through."

"Mackay did what he had to," she fired back, cheeks flushing as she grew angry.

"If you go out there, you're pissing on his memory, on his sacrifice."

"Me?" she said with a disgusted sneer. "What about you?"

"What do you mean?"

"Look at you. You're a mess. Do you think Mackay would want to see you living like this? A worthless hermit who's slowly drinking himself to death."

"He'd understand. I lost everything."

"We both lost a lot!" She screamed. "I saw Dexter murdered, I lost my credibility in the science world, I lost my *career*. Do you see me moping around feeling sorry for myself?"

"Don't try to sell me that self-pity shit. You gained more than anyone from what happened."

"You mean the book?"

"Of course I do. I pleaded with you, begged you not to write it, that no good would come of it, and you just went ahead anyway. That book of yours is what killed our relationship."

"No, Henry, that was all you," she snapped. "I couldn't handle the drinking and the excuses and the misery. You didn't want to let me get over it. You didn't want to let me move forward. The book was my escape."

"No coincidence that it made you an overnight celebrity," he grunted, "all at our expense."

"So the book made money, so what? Writing it was the only way I could cope."

"You could have come to me, you could have talked to me if-"

"How? You were never there for me. Whenever I wanted to talk or tell you how I felt you didn't want to know. We were together but I was alone."

"You profited from what happened to us, you profited on the death of Dexter, and Mackay, hell even Russo and his men. You were selfish."

"Selfish?" She said, striding towards him, teeth gritted. "You dare call me selfish? Who was the one who wouldn't get a job? Who was the one who burned through all my money so he could sit around the house drinking himself into oblivion and feeling sorry for himself? Who was it who told me I couldn't have friends over to the house?"

"I didn't have friends over. Nobody wanted to know."

"That's because you alienated everyone and became a recluse. Just look in the mirror for Christ's sake. You're fat, you stink, and you look a mess. This was the only future I had to look forward to with you and yes, I'll admit, I got out whilst I could, and you know what? It was the best thing I ever did."

"So you make a nice living for yourself off the back of something we were all involved with, don't offer to spread the wealth and then blame me for being bitter?"

"Why would I give you money? To see you piss it all away and hammer another nail into your coffin?"

"I can handle it. I know what I'm doing," he muttered.

"That's all you ever say. It's always, I *know what I'm doing*, everything *will be fine*, or *I'll stop drinking tomorrow*. You're full of shit."

"I don't need this," he said, striding across to the filthy kitchenette. He took a bottle of cheap vodka from the cupboard and unscrewed the cap, taking a drink straight from the bottle.

"Is this what you've become?" she said, striding after him. "I can see your hands shaking. You're drinking yourself into an early grave."

"Like I said, I can handle it."

Without realising she was going to do it, she knocked the bottle out of his hand. It smashed on the hardwood floor.

"Why would you do that?" Henry shouted, disregarding the broken glass as he fell to his knees and started to suck the Vodka up straight from the floor. "This is my last bottle, I don't have any more," he whined.

Despite her anger, a tremendous sadness welled up inside her at just how far Rainwater had fallen. She watched him trying to drink vodka from the filthy floor and thought it would be a miracle if he lasted another year.

"I have to go. I just wanted to tell you face to face what I was doing."

"Please, don't do this," he said, watching as she walked to the door.

She looked at him on his hands and knees, beard wet and dripping onto the floor, eyes wild and yet somehow pleading.

"It's too late. I already agreed to work with Andrews. My publisher wants a second book. This will be perfect material."

"Remember what happened last time. You know how dangerous this thing is. Please... think about what you're about to do. I don't want to lose you."

Her eyes were stinging and her lip began to tremble. As determined as she had been not to show weakness in front of him, a tear rolled down her cheek.

"You lost me a long time ago, Henry," she said quietly, and then left the apartment, closing the door behind her. She waited in the hallway, half hoping he would rush after her and say something else. When he didn't come, she took a deep breath and left the building, wondering when the call would come to say Rainwater had died. Based on his current condition, she didn't think it would be too far away.

CHAPTER FOURTEEN

The custom built four man submersible glided through the chilly Antarctic waters. The silver structure was emblazoned with the initials C.D. on the side for its owner, billionaire, Charles Decker. Something of a playboy and wannabe adventurer, Decker had already invested millions into the project. Some would raise eyebrows at the astronomical costs involved, yet to Decker, it was pocket change. With a personal fortune of just over six billion dollars, he could afford to throw his millions around. The titanium sub neared its target as the pilot navigated closer to the imposing Ross Ice Shelf.

"We're approaching the location now, sir," the pilot said.

"Good, steady now," Decker said, barely able to hide his grin.

Nobody was surprised when Decker decided to go in the sub himself, despite the danger it posed. Those who knew him would have laughed and shrugged, and said it was 'just like Charles', which indeed it was. The thirty nine year old peered out of the porthole window at the icy waters beyond. Born in England in the mid-seventies, he grew up in a hardworking middle class home. Even as a young boy, he had a drive and determination to succeed, however, his fortune came quite by accident. As an eighteen year old university student looking for something to do between classes, he started to work for a local electronics company. Realising quickly the company wasn't operating as efficiently as it could be, the outspoken Decker told his superiors where their failings were. When they didn't act in his suggestions, he directly contacted the company CEO, and painstakingly told him where his company was performing inefficiently and how it could be remedied.

Not liking to be told how to run their family business of the last thirty years by a wet behind the ears new employee, Decker found himself out of a job. Rather than get angry, he set out to prove a point, and using what little savings he had, started his own rival company. Within three years, Decker's company went from a staff of one and being run out of the spare bedroom of his family home, to purchasing its first factory. Now, some twenty one years later, Decker had factories all over the globe producing electronics and military grade weaponry. He had several exclusive and lucrative contracts with the British and American government to provide bespoke equipment. A millionaire by twenty, a billionaire for the first time by twenty seven, Decker had proven just how far drive and determination can take a person. He had grown his fortune wisely, investing in several businesses the world over, as well as an English Premier League football team and a Formula one team whose cars bore his company logo on the bodywork.

It was through his government contact that he had been told what may or may not rest beneath the Ross Ice Shelf. Sure enough, it wasn't the agreed deal, as his informant was supposed to secure him a DNA sample of the creature, which the American government had in captivity. As happens sometimes, plans changed, and Decker was instead given precise coordinates as to where the original incident took place. He had seen the news of the collapse of course on television. However, unlike most, he had paid great attention to the sightings and reports of the alleged sea monster that had been responsible for several deaths. Then in a scene straight out of a Bruce Willis action movie - had been sealed into its lair by a controlled demolition of the Ross Ice Shelf.

Decker always had a great interest in the supernatural, or things that defied known sciences. He had recently funded (and led) an expedition to the Congo to see if the local stories of Mokele Mbembe, and alleged living breathing dinosaur roaming the dense forests, were true. That mission brought no results apart from a few strange sounds heard in the night and a nasty case of dysentery. He was also funding research into proving the existence of life after death, and negotiating with the Turkish government to try to get permission to do a complete search and scan of Mount Ararat to prove once and for all, if the stories of Noah's Ark coming to rest there after the great flood were true.

This particular mission, however, was the one he was most interested in, mostly because he had a very credible source who said the creature existed without question. The file provided by Decker's contact was full of incredibly captivating information, and contained a full account of what had happened. As Decker read it, his heart sank a little. It read too much like a fictional story. It spoke of the project leader, a man called Russo, who lost his mind and went into business for himself, and of not one, but three creatures. The report said Russo wanted to capture one of the young, and it was at this point when things took a turn for the worse. A rival team - the contact said they were fishermen who were also seeking the creature - interrupted the plan and a scuffle broke out leading to an evacuation and the deliberate detonation of the roof of the cave, killing creature and young in the process. Decker was laughing it off when he turned the page and saw the photographs, which in an instant made him think that perhaps there was some truth to the story. There were three in all. One was obviously a still taken from a video. It showed an immense object launching out of the water about to intercept a breaching whale. The scale was unbelievable. It was clear the creature wasn't anything known to science. Its body was a mottled greenish grey, and thick tentacles lined the edges of its frame. In the bottom corner of the photo, hand written in black ink was:

43505986BS44
PROJ BLUE
O/MIST ENCOUNTER
UNVERIFIED

With his heart trip hammering against his ribcage, Decker looked at the other photographs. Both were taken in what looked to be the creature's lair. The grainy image showed a gargantuan bowl of water, and on the edge, a smaller version of the creature from the first photo. Due to his interest in the subject, Decker had seen his share of fakes. In a world of Photoshop, it was very easy to make realistic looking forgeries if someone had the skill. However, this photo looked...right. It looked real. It wasn't designed to show the creature in frightening pose or from deliberately arty camera angles. It looked exactly like it was - an obviously quick photograph taken in the heat of the moment without wanting to be detected.

The third photo was similar, but from a wider angle, and showed people in the cave, agents armed with weapons and clad in snow gear. The creature was still visible at the water's edge, but also beyond a huge wake in the water. This photo had been written on in the same hand. Above the wake in the water, was written: *Adult female.*

Even more interestingly, was the man at the forefront of the image. He was in profile, and looked to be shouting orders as he pointed at the creature. Above him, written in pen was a single word.

Russo.

The man who the government had insisted never existed when Decker had queried, the man who for all intents and purposes, was an enigma, a ghost.

It was enough to spur Decker into action. If the government were so unwilling to talk, then he would take matters into his own hands and go look for himself. The submersible had been specifically designed for this one project at a cost of almost three hundred million dollars. He had hired the best staff. The submersible pilot was a veteran of several high pressure dives including numerous visits to the wreck of the Titanic. Decker's plan was simple. He wanted to see if there was still a way into the alleged underwater cave, and if so, he wanted to go in and look for himself.

"I don't see anything," Decker said, cupping his hands to see through the tiny window.

"Look on the screen," the pilot said, speaking perfect English despite being French.

Decker shifted position in the cramped sub, his arms brushing against the arrays of wires that covered the interior.

"See there?" the captain said, pointing to the screen.

Decker could see it. The video feed came from the high powered cameras mounted at the front of the sub. In missions that relied on greater depths, they were quite useless and couldn't penetrate the blanket of darkness in the deep. For the shallows, however, they delivered a fantastic panorama of the crisp blue ocean. On the screen, the base of the Ross Ice Shelf met with the ocean floor. Majestic for its sheer size, Decker had to remind himself that he was underwater and not in outer space. In the centre of the screen, the evidence of the collapse was plain to see. Rocks dislodged from the seabed had been thrown away from the impact. Where the ice had fallen into the ocean, a ridge of rock was visible, and there, running down it and stretching up towards the surface, was the enormous crack in the rock face.

"If there's a cave entrance, that's where it is, Mr Decker," the pilot said, rolling his 'r's as only the French could.

"Can we get inside?" Decker said.

"Not in the sub, no. It's not safe. With the R.O.Vs, I believe we can take a look."

The R.O.V was a unit first put into use during dives to the wreck of the Titanic. Piloted remotely from the safety of the sub, the small rectangular units were fitted with high resolution cameras, lights, and a retractable mechanical arm. A miniature sub in itself, it was a brilliantly efficient solution for going into those places humans couldn't. For the Titanic missions, they had been able to venture deep into the superstructure of the wreck, exploring areas, which would have otherwise remained inaccessible.

Decker had taken the basic design and improved it. His version of the units had been reshaped for better aerodynamic efficiency and manoeuvrability. He had also managed to cut the weight of the units down by a third, and increase the battery life almost to double its initial capacity.

The unit was tethered to the sub by a thin fibre optic cable so that in the event of power loss, the units could be reeled back to the submersible manually.

"Mr Decker, should I release the R.O.V?" the pilot said, half turning towards the billionaire.

"Yes, but I want to pilot it."

"Mr Decker, I understand your excitement, but surely an experienced pilot would be better."

"I've trained. I had a simulator built at my home."

"Oui, Mr Decker, but I must stress how different a real world setting is. Ocean currents, unexpected rock falls, the chance of snagging the cable on something and getting hung up. The cost to replace these units is-"

"Something I can easily afford, Jacques. Remember, I'm financing this entire trip. If there's something in that cave, I want to be first to discover it."

"Oui, monsieur. My apologies," the Frenchman said.

Beneath the monitor display were two joystick controls used to pilot the R.O.V unit. One stick controlled pitch, the other lateral motion. There were also buttons to control forward or reverse thrust of the twin propellers at the rear of the unit. Decker took a deep breath and grasped the joysticks firmly.

"Okay, power up the unit," he said. The pilot complied, flicking an array of switches and referring to readouts on a small screen to his right.

"Unit is operational. Test rudder and thrust, please, Mr Decker."

Decker complied.

"Okay," the pilot said, "switching to R.O.V camera view."

The screen changed to a view of the belly of the sub covering the top two thirds of the screen, reminding Decker of the opening scene of the first Star Wars movie.

"Disengaging holding clamps," the pilot said, flicking another switch.

The image on screen shuddered, and then the belly of the sub started to drift off the top of the screen as the R.O.V was released.

"Okay, monsieur Decker, you have control," the pilot said.

"Understood," Decker replied, concentrating all his efforts on screen and remembering to remain supple and calm, teasing the controls and moving the unit towards the crack in the rock face.

"I'm impressed, Mr Decker, you have a skilled hand," the pilot said as he watched the screen.

"Just like playing computer games, Jacques."

"Only more expensive, no?"

Decker grinned and banked the unit towards the crack in the rock face.

"This looks like it's been here for years," Decker muttered. "I wonder if this is where our creature got in and out."

"You really think it's there?" Jacques said.

"I wouldn't have spent so much money if I didn't."

"I hope you aren't too disappointed."

"Worth every penny to know one way or the other, my friend. Better than the great unknown."

Decker piloted the unit into the crevasse, switching on the lights as he did. "Just as I thought," he said as he dived deeper. "The cave entrance was through the rock rather than the ice. We might yet have a chance to see something."

The cave walls were wide, digging into the earth before tapering into the ice. Decker piloted the R.O.V to where the walls narrowed and brought it to a halt.

"Unbelievable," Jacques said, unable to help grinning. "You see how it opens again on the other side?"

"Yeah, it shows why our creature got in, but couldn't get out if it's as big as they said. As soon as it reached maturity, it simply wouldn't have fit once it reached a certain size. It must have been trapped until the first collapse freed it."

"Can you pan up, Mr Decker?" Jacques said.

Decker did as he was asked. They could now clearly see the join between seafloor and ice, the sheer rock giving way seamlessly to the shelf. Directly above them, the evidence of the cave collapse was evident.

"You see that, Jacques? I'm betting there might well be some structure intact if we can get in. It looks to be like the base of the body of water in which this thing made its lair, was built around the seabed rather than the ice." He panned the R.O.V back level. "If we can go in here through the crack in the rock, we should be able to ascend and see if there is anything left to see."

"You mean descend, monsieur Decker," Jacques corrected. "Anything left would be on the floor now, no?"

"You're right, of course," Decker said. "Why don't we go and take a look."

Decker piloted the sub into the darkness, flicking the high powered lights across the front of the unit on to full power. The ocean came back to life, the lights barely penetrating the gloom.

"Careful, Mr Decker. Do you see the evidence of the collapse? There, to the right?"

"Yeah, I see it," Decker said under his breath, banking away from the huge boulder of ice which Jacques referred to. Palms sweating, Decker hesitated for a moment, watching the swirling microbes and algae as it danced across the illuminated field of view. "Okay, let's see what we can see."

Decker pushed the nose of the R.O.V down, moving forward at a descending angle towards the floor. All around he could see evidence of the collapse and the tremendous forces of nature that had been at work.

"Jesus, would you look at this," Decker muttered. "Those ice blocks are the size of houses. They've been tossed around with ease."

"Be careful, it looks tight up ahead," Jacques said.

"I see it. Hang on."

Decker teased the controls, turning the R.O.V on its side and going under a horizontal block of ice. Beyond, the field of view opened beyond the reach of the miniature sub's lights.

"I think we're in," Decker said, unable to hide the smile, which grew on one side of his face.

"Yes, this is it!" Jacques said, also struggling to hide his excitement. "You reached the cave."

"Now, let's see if we can find our creature."

Decker went slowly, inching as close to the bottom as he could amid the huge boulders of rock and ice, which littered what, used to be the natural bowl of the creature's lair.

"It seems like apart from the initial debris, the bulk of the roof collapse left most of the underwater area untouched," Decker said as he moved around a particularly large ice formation. The water is so cold in here that the ice doesn't melt."

"Could it be possible this creature survived?" Jacques said, glancing wide eyed at Decker.

"Unlikely. Look at the debris all over the bottom. As big as it was, I don't think-"

Decker stopped speaking, staring at the screen.

"Merde," Jacques mumbled, as he too stared in astonishment.

It was only partially visible, most of its lower three quarters crushed under an immense pile of ice. The forward portion of the creature was devoid of skin, its bones standing out in stark white in the glare of the sub's lights. Even devoid of flesh, the size of the animal was almost impossible to comprehend. It was plain to see it was a force of nature, and for the first time, Decker was grateful it was dead. He piloted the sub closer to the gargantuan skull, which was on its side, half buried in silt and rock.

"Those teeth," Jacques mumbled.

"I see them. What do you think, fifteen, maybe twenty inches long?"

"More. I'd say twenty five."

"I'm going to try to snag one," Decker said, pausing to wipe his hands on his pale blue jumpsuit. "Deploying the mechanical arm."

Decker flicked a switch. From the underbelly of the R.O.V, the three pronged stainless steel appendages extended into view on screen.

"Okay, I'm moving into position," Decker said, then turned towards the watching pilot. "Jacques, would you operate the arm? I never did get the hang of it."

"Of course, Monsieur Decker. Please switch control over to me."

Decker flipped a switch, giving the pilot control of the retractable arm from a secondary console.

"Oaky, I'll keep her steady," Decker said, a light sweat forming on his brow. "The bones have been down here for a while now, so you should be able to dislodge one of the teeth from the jawbone easily enough."

Jacques didn't answer. Instead, he manipulated the appendage with much more grace and Dexterity than Decker would have ever been able to. The billionaire watched as the three pronged arm wrapped around one of the teeth. Jacques manipulated the controls, and the arm moved up and down, trying to pry the tooth free.

"It's not moving, we need more leverage," Jacques said.

"Okay, maintain grip. On three, pull back. I'll pull the R.O.V up at the same time. That should give us the leverage we need."

"Yes, Mr Decker, understood."

"Oaky, are you ready?"

"Oui."

"Alright, here we go. On three. One. Two. Three. Pull!"

In perfect synchronisation, both men pulled back on their respective controls. The tooth popped free as the R.O.V ascended, bumping into the ice above the creature's skull. The impact skewed the mini sub, causing the arm to lose its grip on the tooth, which sank towards the floor.

"Shit, don't lose it," Decker said as he recovered and stabilised the vehicle.

"It's okay, I see it," Jacques said. "There, by the first vertebrae."

Decker looked where the Frenchman was pointing on screen.

"Yep, I see it. Good eye, Jacques."

Decker lowered the nose and inched towards the enormous skull and the prize they had almost lost. The Frenchman extended the mechanical arm, and with graceful ease, picked up the tooth.

"Got it," he said, grinning at Decker.

"Fantastic work, you just earned yourself one hell of a bonus," Decker said. "Just don't lose it."

"Merci, Mr Decker. The tooth will be quite safe until we reach the surface. The R.O.V has a sample box in its underbelly. It will be safe there until we are back on board the Emerald."

"Excellent. A successful mission all around," Decker said.

"Mister Decker, forgive me for asking, but what will you do now you have the tooth?"

Decker smiled. "Jacques, in this world, you can have all the money in the world and still be powerless without a little thing called leverage, and that tooth, my Gaelic friend, is a great big chunk of it."

"But still, what will you do?"

"Whatever I want to Jacques," Decker replied with a smile, "whatever the hell I want to."

CHAPTER FIFTEEN

Back at the motel, the mood hadn't been improved by the trip to the bar. Jim sat on one of the two beds, staring at the television screen. Marie had returned to her position on the floor and she had been joined by Fernando. Joanne and Tom were on the other bed, also watching the news. There was no desire to speak. All of them knew the situation even if they were no closer to knowing what to do about it. Although they had all had a little to drink, it was only Jim who had indulged himself, and was glassy eyed as he stared through the television to whatever private oblivion he was imagining.

The news crews were now reporting from both locations. One crew was at the beach, the other by the roadside where the driver had been killed. Both scenes were taped off and surrounded by crowds of rubberneckers who were trying to get a look at the grisly view.

"I wish they'd show something else already," Tom said as he adjusted position.

"They won't," Joanne replied. "This is big news around here."

"It still doesn't help us to figure out what we're gonna do," Fernando interjected.

"For now we should just-"

There was a knock on the door.

Worried glances were exchanged as Tom started to get off the bed.

"No, ignore it," Jim whispered.

"I can't, they'll know we're in here. The TV and the lights will give us away."

"It could be anyone though, it's too risky."

"It will look more suspicious if we don't answer. Everyone just stay calm," Tom said as he crossed the room.

He took a moment to compose himself, gave a final glance to the others, and then opened the door.

Tom immediately recognised the man from the bar. He was

distinct enough anyway as is, without the obvious disability of the missing hand.

"You're those kids from the bar," the man said, his accent heavy Australian.

"Did you follow us here?" Tom said as Fernando and Joanne joined him at the door.

"Yeah, I followed you."

"Why?"

"Why d'ya think?" Greg said with a half-smile.

"Sorry, you have the wrong people," Joanne said, reaching past Tom and starting to close the door.

"I don't think so, girly," Greg said. "I don't think so at all."

"If you don't go away, we'll be forced to call the police," she countered.

"Come on," he said, "we both know you won't do that."

"Buddy, you don't know shit," Tom said.

"I know more than you think. For example, I know that whatever was on that trailer you stole, wasn't a whale like they're saying on the news."

"Look, I'm sorry, but we don't know what you're talking about," Joanne said.

"No, maybe *you* don't, but he does," Greg replied, pointing at Tom. "I can see it in his eyes. He knows what he's done, what kind of thing he's set free, don't you?"

Tom looked at Joanne, too shocked to formulate a response.

"If you kids really wanna know what it is you're dealing with, you better let me in. Unless of course, you want to get into it right here on the doorstep."

"What do you know about it?" Tom said.

Greg held up his stump. "I know it well enough. Let's just say that for now."

"Alright, you better come in."

"Tom!"

"No, Joanne. It's obvious he knows about this. Maybe he can help us."

"You should listen to your friend," Greg said, grinning at Joanne. "Believe me, you're gonna want to hear this."

With nothing else to say, Greg walked into the motel room. He turned the wooden chair at the dresser around to the face the inquisitive group and sat down. The others perched on the bed, watching and waiting to see what would be said. Greg looked at them each in turn, trying to figure out if they actually knew the magnitude of what they had done.

"Look, pal, you better start talking fast about who you are and what you know," Jim said, his agitation plain to see.

"Hold your horses, kid. I'm getting to it," Greg said, taking another few seconds to gather his thoughts. Finally ready, he went on. "The name's Michaels. Greg Michaels. Five years ago, I had a thriving shark fishing business. I had a life, I was getting by, or at least I was until I had an encounter with one of those things you freed. In the end, it cost me my business, my hand, and any worthwhile aspect of my life. I had my suspicions the government would have something to do with it. This just proves my point. Now, you lot are responsible for lettin' this thing loose."

"Look, take a step back. You're rushing ahead here," Tom said, glancing at the others. "You need to explain."

"I'll explain alright, and then we all need to talk about what happens next."

Greg waited for any protest, and then continued, recalling the memories with ease.

"It happened when I took a client with the intention of going shark spotting off the coast of Australia..."

For the next thirty minutes, Greg told his story, leaving out nothing, giving every detail as he remembered it. For the duration of his account, the others watched, captivated by the horrific scenes as Greg described them. It was the first time he had spoken out loud about what had happened, and he found that to say it, cut him even deeper than just the memories. He finished his account, and waited to see how the others would react. Fernando was the one who spoke first, his voice barely loud enough to hear.

"We didn't know. I mean, how could we have known?"

"No good feeling sorry now, kid. It's done, and this thing is free."

"Look, Mr Michaels, I'm sorry for what happened to you, I really am. You have to understand this isn't our fault," Tom said.

"Never said it was."

"So, what happens now? Are you going to turn us in to the police?" Joanne asked.

The others watched and waited, all apart from Jim who was thinking about the flip knife in his jeans and how quickly he could get to it. However, any course of action was diverted by Greg's next words.

"No, I'm not gonna turn you in."

"So, what is it you want from us?" Tom said.

"Isn't it obvious?"

"Look, if it's blackmail, you're wasting your time. We don't have any money and-"

"Relax, Girly, it's not blackmail," Greg said with a grin, cutting Joanne off. "What I want from you is help. Help to put this right. I want you to come with me and kill this thing."

"Thanks for the offer," Tom said with a half-smile, "but we don't want any part of this. We're already in enough trouble as it is. Best of luck though."

Something changed in Greg's face then. It may have been something as simple as a trick of the light, or maybe it was the way his eyes took on a darkness. Whatever it was, it was enough to scare Tom into silence.

"I don't think you understand," Greg said quietly. "I wasn't giving you an option. You people *will* help me to kill this thing. You were responsible for letting it loose, and as stupid as that was, this gives me the perfect chance to get my revenge."

"Who the hell do you think you are? You can't force us to do shit," Jim said.

"I wouldn't be so sure," Greg fired back, swelling in confidence. "See, I have a buddy of mine waiting outside. He's just waiting to call the police and tell them everything about you. He's very thorough. He even took photos of you as you were leaving the bar. If you refuse to help me, you won't get five miles before every copper in America is looking for you."

"You're bluffing," Joanne said without conviction.

"Maybe I am, maybe I'm not. You can all choose to ignore me and throw me out of this room right now in the hope that you're right, but if I were you, I don't think I'd want to take that chance.

Jesus, if you think it's scary having to hide out now, imagine what it will be like when your faces are plastered all over the news. You won't even be able to take a shit without wondering if someone's gonna kick the door down and arrest you."

"Please, you can't make us do this," Tom said. "We need to hide out, lay low. You have to see it from our point of view."

"I sympathise, I really do. Doesn't change a thing though."

"Please, you can't ask us to do this. We don't even have a boat," Fernando said.

"I have. Way I see it; it's as good a place as any to hide out for a while. It must be better than sitting around in here and wondering how long it will be before they find you."

"What if we refuse?" Jim said. Unlike the others, he didn't seem afraid. If anything, he looked angry.

Keep an eye on this one.

Greg heeded the inner warning as he replied. "As I said, it's up to you. As the girly said, I could well be bluffing. Then again, you have to ask yourself why would I? Unlike you, I don't have anything to lose. Seems to me like finding and killing this fish would be a big step towards righting some wrongs. To me, I say that gives us some common ground to work on."

"Look, Mr Michaels-"

"Greg."

"Look, Greg," Tom went on, "this is a big decision. You can't expect us just to give you an answer right away. We need some time to think."

"Of course you do, I understand that," Greg said, standing and setting the chair back at the dresser. He reached into his jacket and pulled out a folded scrap of paper. "That's where my boat is. It's called the Sea Star. End of the dock. Take a little while to think things through. If you're not there by six am, I'll assume you have declined my offer. When that happens, I'll have no option but to inform the authorities where you are."

"Six am? That's only a few hours from now. It's not enough time for us to decide." Fernando whined. "Why the big rush?"

"Because we need to act now. If we wait any longer, then this fish is gonna grow to its full size, and then we're gonna have a *real* problem."

Greg walked to the door and opened it, then turned back to face the group. "You might be tempted to take your chances and run. I know I would be. If that's what you decide, then I can't stop you. I just hope you have a damn good place to go."

"Why?" Tom asked.

"Well, it seems to me you busted open a government secret. People are already asking questions and they'll want a scapegoat so they don't tarnish their image. Do you think they'll have a problem pinning it on a bunch of dumb kids like you lot?"

"But it was an accident," Marie said, voice wavering. "We didn't know it would happen like this."

Fernando grabbed her hand. "She's right, we didn't know."

"Hey, for the record, I believe you," Greg said, "but you can bet your ass they won't. They'll catch you and make an example of you. A warning to others not to fuck with them."

He looked at them for a few seconds more, letting the words sink in. "Anyway, think about it. Six o clock. If you don't show, at six oh-one, your faces become national news."

With that, he left, closing the door behind him. Of course, he didn't have their photographs, or someone waiting in the wings to expose them for who they were. He was, however, a hell of a good liar. It had served him well over the years, and he was sure it had done so again. For all the bravado, he could see they were just kids who had gotten in too deep. There was no guilt in using that to his advantage. It seemed fate had actually stopped kicking him in the balls for once, and had given him an opportunity finally to get some vengeance for the misery that had filled his life for the last few years. As much as he tried to deny it, he had been dead inside for a long time apart from the thirst for revenge. It burned deep, and he knew even if it meant going to extremes, he would do it in order to get the job done.

CHAPTER SIXTEEN

Rainwater clung to the toilet bowl, panting as his mouth started to water. He always hated this, the few seconds before he knew there was nothing to stop the oncoming vomit. He knew the reason of course. Too little food combined with too much drink. He tightened his grip on the bowl as he felt it come, the vomit preceded by more mouth-watering. Without ceremony, he threw up the contents of his stomach into the less than clean toilet bowl. When he was done, he glanced down at the murky water. There was blood mixed in with the stuff he had ejected. Not much, granted, but enough for him to realise things had to change. He sat there, resting his head against the cool porcelain and tried to figure out if the decision he had made was the right one. It was a life changer. That was for sure, but at the same time, based on the bloody water by his head, it was one he had to make.

There was a knock on the door, three sharp rapports. Rainwater's heart sank. He couldn't handle another argument with Clara, not after the one the previous day had ended with him desperately sucking vodka off the floor like some shameless alcoholic - which he supposed he was. Either way, the shame at letting her see him in such a way had been behind his decision finally to do something about it.

The knock came again. Although he desperately wanted to ignore it, he also wanted a chance to explain himself and put things right. Dragging himself up and flushing away the mess, he staggered to the door and threw it open.

Andrews stood at the other side. Rainwater cursed himself for not checking who it was before he answered. He had no desire to speak to anyone, especially Andrews. He was still angry at what had happened, and wasn't sure he could hold back from attacking if Andrews did anything to further goad him.

"She's not here," Rainwater said, leaning against the doorframe.

"I know that. Can I come in?"

"What do you want?"

"Just to talk."

"I've got nothing to say to you."

"Please, just give me five minutes."

With a sigh, Rainwater stood aside and let Andrews in.

"Clara told me what happened," He said as he looked around the filthy apartment.

"She told you her version of events you mean. You bastards really did a job of convincing her to go."

"Actually, she jumped at the chance. She had every opportunity to back out but didn't take it. She's ambitious."

"She's stupid, and you are too if you're going out there."

Rainwater walked to his bed. There was an open case at the foot of it. Andrews followed, watching Rainwater as he packed his clothes.

"I came here to see if I could talk you into changing your mind. It looks like I might not have to."

"Don't get too excited, it's not what you think."

"So what is it?" Andrews pressed.

Rainwater turned to face him "It's none of your business."

"Wait a second; don't tell me you're going out there alone like last time."

Rainwater grinned without humour. "Jesus, you really don't know me at all do you? Like I told Clara, I'm done with this. I won't be a part of it. You don't have to worry about me getting under your feet out there. Trust me; I'm going nowhere near it."

"So where *are* you going?"

Rainwater stopped packing, dropping a sweater into his case and looking Andrews in the eye. "I'd tell you to mind your own business, but I know how you government types have a habit of finding things out. If you really want to know, I'm getting out of here. I need to get away and get my life back on track."

"Where will you go? Back to Alaska?"

Rainwater shook his head. "No. Too many memories there. I need a completely clean break."

"Where then?"

"England."

"England?" Andrews repeated. "That's a little extreme isn't it? We could really use your help on this. If not for me, for Clara."

"Forget it. It's already decided."

"What the hell's so special about England? Why there?"

"Because it's not here," Rainwater said. "Hell, I'm not stupid. I know how much of a mess I am. What my life has become. If I came with you I'd be a liability."

"But Clara-"

"Clara has made her decision. I know her enough to understand she's stubborn enough not to change her mind now."

"Can you at least give me an address? Let me know where you'll be if we need to contact you?"

"No," Rainwater said. "That's the whole point. I want to get away from your reach. I want to be left alone."

"To do what?" Andrews countered. "Drink yourself to death?"

"No. To get cleaned up. I need to make a change."

"Okay, how about this. You come along to assist us, and I guarantee the government will put you through the very best rehab money can buy. We both know you can't do it alone."

Rainwater shook his head. "You know, it never surprises me how little people think of me."

"It's not an insult," Andrews countered. "I used to really respect you, which is why I'll give it to you straight now."

"Go on then, let me hear it."

"Bottom line is, it doesn't matter if it's England, Alaska, or anywhere else in the world. We both know you can't quit. You're an addict, Henry, and for an addict, it's always tomorrow."

"No, you're wrong."

"No, I'm not. There will always be an excuse. There will always be a reason to start tomorrow. If you really, genuinely want to get back on track, help us. In return, I'll personally drive you to rehab and make sure you get better."

Rainwater hesitated. He didn't trust Andrews, yet, was half tempted to believe him all the same. "Nice try." He said, closing and zipping his suitcase.

"Henry, this is a mistake. Your experience will be invaluable."

"This is your monster now, not mine."

"Is there nothing I can say to convince you?"

"No. Not a thing," Rainwater said.

"Then if you won't give me a means to contact you, let me at least give one to you." He reached into his pocket and handed

Rainwater a folded piece of paper. "That's my direct number. If, and when you get to England and you change your mind, call me."

"Alright, I won't, but if it will get you to leave me alone, I'll take the damn number." Rainwater said as he took the card from Andrews.

"Well, I suppose I better let you finish packing," Andrews said, walking towards the door.

"Hey, Andrews," Rainwater called across the room.

"Yeah?"

"Do me a favour."

"What?"

"Clara. Bring her back safe. Don't forget how dangerous this thing is."

"I'll do my best. Don't lose that number, you hear?"

"Yeah. I hear you."

Andrews opened the door, and then turned back. "Good luck out there, Henry. I really hope you find what you're looking for."

Andrews closed the door before Rainwater could respond. Rainwater looked around the apartment and let out a long sigh. "Yeah, me too," he muttered under his breath.

CHAPTER SEVENTEEN

The 42 foot, 45,000 lb Whale Shark drifted through the warm waters of the Ningaloo Reef, just off the coast of Western Australia. Despite its size, the Whale Shark wasn't a predator like its kin the Great White. Instead, it was a filter feeder, making up its diet of Microalgae, krill, and plankton. One of only three species of filter feeder in the world, along with the Basking and Megamouth shark, it was a gentle giant of the seas.

After being freed off the coast of Florida, the creature had been aimless in roaming the seas, its senses overcome with stimulus, which it felt compelled to investigate. After spending some time in the colder Antarctic waters, it had followed a pod of migrating whales towards the temperate blue waters of the Indian Ocean. There it had homed in on the vibrations of the Whale Shark as it sucked in another huge mouthful of seawater, filtering it out through the gills and retaining the plankton and other microorganisms.

Now at almost a hundred and twenty feet in length, the creature had developed an almost insatiable hunger. Unlike its parent, which had spent much of its life trapped inside the ice cave, the offspring had become used to regular feeds during its captivity, and had retained that routine since its escape. It had already feasted on numerous squid, whales and sharks, and yet, was never satisfied.

The slow moving giant Whale Shark detected the creature as it drew closer, for now retaining its distance. Due to its size, the Whale Shark usually had no natural predators, and was hardly equipped to fight.

With hunger driving it forward, the creature flicked its tail, closing to within a few hundred feet of the shark. Hoping its size would prove the necessary intimidation, the Whale Shark didn't flee, but faced its potential attacker head on.

Rising to the challenge, the creature charged, accelerating towards its target and opening its giant jaws ready to strike. The creature spasmed as a great jolt of pain speared through its body. Abandoning its potential meal, and leaving the Whale Shark to its own devices, the confused creature went deep as another surge of pain lit it up from within. Skimming along the seafloor, the creature came across an underwater cave system. Plunging into the darkness, another jolt caused it to smash against the side of the cave wall. It circled erratically above the floor of the cave. Another jolt of agony overcame the creature as it pushed out a pale white egg, which was almost eight feet in diameter. Unable to resist its instinctive urge, the creature snapped at the blood, which clouded the water. More pain heralded another egg, then a third. For the next five hours, the sequence repeated. When it was done, the exhausted creature lay on the cave floor surrounded by more than thirty eggs. Much like the seahorse, the asexual creature needed no companion to reproduce, only a suitable location in which to spawn. Declaring the cave and surrounding waters as its territory, the creature set out to find food and rid the waters of any creatures it deemed to be a threat to its domain.

RETURN TO THE DEEP

CHAPTER EIGHTEEN

Washington Harbour
Washington DC

The one hundred and forty foot vessel looked distinctly average as it bobbed against the dock, which was of course a quite deliberate design choice made by the United States government. Underneath the unassuming fibreglass hull, the ship was fitted with the very latest and most advanced in underwater radar and detection systems.

With more than a little trepidation, Andrews made his way down the dock to where it waited. He still couldn't quite believe it had come to this again. Flashbacks of his time spent with Russo almost made him request someone else take the mission, and yet, he knew he would hate that even more, just sitting in an office and having no real control over what happened. Like it or not, this way was best.

He looked at the people around him as he walked down the dockside, civilians clad in shorts and sunglasses, laughing and relaxing without a care in the world. He wished he could have that, and was envious at their happy go lucky nature as they enjoyed what was shaping up to be a beautiful day.

He could see the boat ahead, and his gut tightened a little, even more so when he saw what was happening on it. There were people swarming over the rear deck with all sorts of equipment. People who shouldn't be there. He increased his pace, eager to find out what's going on. As he got closer to the stern of the boat, he could see Clara giving directions to the three man camera crew on board whilst a fourth loaded on supplies.

"What the hell's going on here?"

"This is my crew," Clara said, pushing her hair behind her ear.

"TV cameras? Are you serious?" Andrews said, glaring at Clara.

"It's been authorised."

"Bullshit it has. I don't know anything about it."

"Then you better check with Tomlinson. He said I could bring a crew."

"Can I have a word with you?" Andrews said, barely able to contain his anger.

"Of course, go right ahead."

"In private."

"No problem," she said, climbing onto the dock.

"Come with me," Andrews said, leading her away from the camera crew, who were now relegated to standing around and looking confused. "What the hell is this? You can't put this on TV."

"It not for TV. It's for research."

"For another goddamn book?" Andrews hissed. "After all the trouble the last one caused."

"It's fiction, and that's exactly how I'll market it. The cameras are just so I can research everything I need to."

"And you seriously expect me to believe that Tomlinson gave the okay for this?"

"Why don't you ask him?" She said with a sneer.

"Alright, I will," Andrews countered, determined to call her bluff.

She waited and watched him as he walked away and made the call, speaking in hushed tones and flashing the occasional killer look in her direction. She simply smiled. As a woman who had become accustomed to getting what she wanted, she wasn't about to let anyone intimidate her. With an expression that could sour milk, she saw Andrews end the call and stride back towards her.

"I don't know how you managed to convince him of this, but he confirmed your agreement."

"I told you he would."

Ignoring the arrogant response, Andrews went on. "You just make sure you tell this crew of yours to keep out of the way. This boat isn't really big enough to house three extra people."

"I was going to ask about that," Clara said. "Why such a small boat? I thought the government would have the big guns out for this."

"With what explanation?" Andrews countered. "Like last time, the government want to avoid embarrassment and more importantly, questions. They decided low key was the way forward."

"And how the hell do you expect to kill this thing when we find it?" She said, a little panic creeping into her voice.

"We don't."

"What do you mean?"

"Our job is to find it, nothing more. As soon as we locate it, we have destroyers and submarines on standby. It's not going to be a mess like last time. This time it'll be swift. No screwing around." Andrews grinned as he said it. "What? Did you expect us to go out all guns blazing and kill this thing in a hundred and forty foot boat?"

"Actually I did," Clara grunted as colour flushed her cheeks. "Why else would you ask me along otherwise?"

"Come on; think about it, you're a smart woman."

"What the hell is that supposed to mean?"

"It means that before you were hobnobbing with those celebrity pals of yours, you were a marine biologist and a damn good one. Plus, you have experience of dealing with this thing before. We don't want Clara Thompson the celebrity author on this trip, but the Clara of old."

"I don't do that anymore. It's not who I am."

"If you want those cameras to roll on your little film to help you write that next best seller, you better get used to the idea. Either way, you'll have to make up your own ending to the story, because you and I will be far away from this fish when the army moves in to finish it off."

"Fine," she said, glaring at him, "I won't go."

"That's up to you," Andrews shrugged.

"I mean it. You need me."

"As usual, you have way too high an opinion of yourself."

"Look, I already told you, I'll leave. I have no issue with not doing this."

Andrews searched her face, and knew she was lying. For as much as she could almost hide it, he could smell the desperation on her. He knew it was important to establish control now before it caused problems at sea.

"Fine," he said as he walked back towards the boat, "everyone off. You with the camera, move it now."

"Wait, what are you doing?" Clara said, jogging to catch up to him. Andrews, however, was ignoring her.

"Hey, are you deaf?" He said to the camera crew, who were looking from Andrews to Clara in obvious confusion. "Grab your shit and get off this boat."

"Alright, you win," Clara said, "I'll help you find this damn fish."

Andrews turned to her, deliberately grinning. "See? It's easy to make the right call if you really think about it. The United States Government thanks you."

"If you had any sense, you would have a tracker on this thing and know exactly where it was."

"We actually do have a tracker on it, but it's only short range."

"Which, in other words means it's useless."

"It was only intended to monitor its location in its tank for safety reasons when we were cleaning the filters and pumps. We never anticipated it would get out into open ocean."

"Great," Clara said. "What kind of range is short range?"

"Couple of miles, maybe less."

"Like I said, less than useless."

"Look, it is what it is."

"A needle in a haystack, that's what it is."

"And that's why you're here," Andrews said. "Now please, if we can just get the hell out of here and start to look for this thing, I'd appreciate it."

"I need half an hour. I want to film an establishing shot of me getting on board the boat."

You arrogant bitch.

Andrews didn't say it, he couldn't be bothered dealing with the hassle. Instead, he sighed and tried to control his anger. "You have ten minutes. Anyone not on board when time's up is staying here. Understood?"

Without giving her a chance to answer, Andrews hopped onto the boat and disappeared inside the wheelhouse.

CHAPTER NINETEEN

As Greg suspected, Tom and the others had arrived as instructed the following morning. They were every bit as nervous and cautious as he expected them to be, and eyed up the thirty two foot boat with more than a little apprehension. The green painted hull was cracked, tired, and spotted with rust. A far cry from the expensive cruiser he used to own, it was all he could afford and although it didn't look it, was just about as sea worthy. They had set out to sea under slate coloured rain heavy skies, the vessel tossed around by the choppy oceans. Greg controlled the vessel with ease, his disability not affecting his ability to function as Tom and his friends sat around the table, watching him carefully.

Tom looked out of the window as the first spots of rain fell, and then turned to Greg. "Why are we staying so close to the coast?"

"We need to make a quick stop off before we head out."

"For what?"

"None of your business."

"I think it is since you brought us along. We deserve to know."

Greg glared at Tom, then slid his eyes to Joanne who sat next to him and was infinitely more subdued than last time he saw her.

"What's the matter with her?" Greg said, avoiding the initial question.

"Nothing."

"Doesn't look like nothing."

"None of your business," Tom said, echoing Greg's earlier comment.

Joanne felt their eyes on her, and stared at her hands, which were folded on the tabletop. She hadn't told the others what was wrong, and for the most part they hadn't asked, assuming she was simply struggling to cope with everything that had happened. She was happy to let them think it because it meant they wouldn't dig around for the truth. She *was* afraid, that much was true, but not of the creature, they were setting out to find.

She was afraid of Jim.

She suspected he had more to do with what had happened on

the beach, and was less than convinced by his version of events that fully implicated Clayton, and left him as the innocent party. She knew well enough the kind of background Jim had. He was a troublemaker, a reckless kid who liked to act first and deal with the consequences later. She knew he came from a violent family, but always gave him the benefit of the doubt. Now however, she was convinced he was responsible for not only the death of the truck driver, but also of Clayton. Even as she sat there on the boat, she could feel Jim's eyes on her, burning into her soul. Flashbacks of the previous night came flooding back, and she had to grip the edge of the table to stop herself from losing it.

After Greg had left the previous night, they had talked for a while, and quickly came to the conclusion that they had no choice but to go along with it. Only Jim objected, saying they should run, and that they could be far enough away so that, if and when, Greg notified the authorities, they would stand a good chance of staying hidden. The rest of the group disagreed, and although he fought it, Jim went along with it. Shortly after, they decided to get a few hours sleep.

Later, with the steady sounds of her sleeping friends all around her, Joanne lay in the dark, too agitated to sleep. They were already in deep, and the way she saw it, things would only get worse. She closed her eyes, trying to will her body to rest and give her some respite, but her brain wasn't playing ball, and fired scenarios and questions at her with distressing regularity.

She heard a sound.

Opening her eyes, she peered into the gloom. She watched as Jim got up from the floor where he had been sleeping, creep to the dresser, grab the bag Joanne had brought with her and take it to the bathroom. She glanced at Tom, who was still sleeping. She reached out a hand to wake him, and then stopped. Instead, she quietly climbed out of bed and walked to the bathroom door. She could see the bar of light flooding under it, and as she put her ear to the wood, could hear him rummaging around, no doubt searching for the money she had brought with them.

Overcome by anger, she opened the door and walked into the room without knowing she was going to do it, closing it behind her.

Jim stared at her as she entered, eyes wide, one arm still inside the bag.

"If you're looking for the money, I moved it," she whispered.

"I wasn't, I was looking for some pain killers or something for this headache."

"Drop the act. I'm on to you."

"What do you mean?" Jim said, still playing innocent.

"You know what I mean. The others might not see it, but I know you had more to do with Clayton's death than you're saying. Wouldn't surprise me if you were the one who shot the driver too."

She expected Jim to flounder, or stutter some kind of explanation, which would further confirm her suspicion. Instead, he slowly removed his hand from the bag and turned towards her. He smiled, the harsh lighting from above throwing his face into a ghoulish mask.

"You should be careful saying things like that," he whispered.

She tried to back away, finding the closed door stopping her. All the bravery had gone now, leaving only fear.

"I'm not afraid of you," she said, trying to convince herself.

"Yes you are," he replied, taking a step towards her.

"What are you going to do?" She asked.

"Me? Nothing," he replied, stretching his smile. "As long as you stop giving me a hard time in front of the others."

"You did it though, didn't you? It was you, not Clayton," she said, unable to keep the waver out of her voice.

He leaned close to her, his nose inches from hers. He reached up and put a hand around her throat, his touch gentle but sinister all the same. "Let's just say I did," he whispered, "that means it wouldn't be hard to do it again if somebody was threatening to tell people."

She was trembling now, unable to stop. She wasn't sure how she had missed it before, but could see now in his eyes that they were bottomless black wells.

"Then go, if that's what you want to do. Run, take the money. Just leave us alone."

"I was going to, but now I'm not so sure."

"Why not?"

He tightened his grip slightly, just enough to make her

uncomfortable. "Because I know what will happen. As soon as I leave, you'll start to talk, you'll make things up."

"I won't, I swear I won't, I-"

"You know what will happen to me? Have you any idea what my dad would do to me if he knew I was involved in all this? I can see him now, sitting at home with his buddies, already half cut and watching the news telling his friends how no son of his would get away with doing something like that."

"And is he right?" Joanne whispered.

"About what?"

"You know what I mean."

"I know, I want you to say it."

Although she was older than he was by five years, the seventeen year old Jim was tall and stocky, and had huge arms and shoulders. There was no mistake that he could easily overpower her. "Did you kill Clayton and that other man?"

He paused, and for a moment, it felt as if the whole world had stopped moving, then without warning, he released his grip on her neck and took a step back. "No. Of course not, but if, for the sake of argument I had, then you might want to tread carefully from here on."

"Why?"

"Because someone who had already gone to those lengths twice before, might be desperate enough to do it again if it meant saving their own skin."

"Is that a threat?" she asked.

"It's a statement. Take it however you want."

He reached past her and grabbed the door handle, hesitating just long enough to make her flinch, then opened it and squeezed past her, leaving her alone in the bathroom.

She hadn't mentioned it to the others, and neither had Jim. Now as they sat on the boat less than five feet from each other, she was more afraid than ever.

"Hey, man," Fernando said, "this boat is way too small. Where the hell will we all sleep?"

"Don't worry about it," Greg grunted.

"Seriously though, there's no way we can all stay here. There's no space."

"Who said we were staying on this boat?" Greg said, grinning at them.

"What do you mean?" Tom said.

"Take a look."

They stood and looked out of the window. Ahead, bobbing on the ocean was a ninety foot white hulled boat, which even from a distance oozed luxury. From the blacked out windows to the name penned in tall script on the bow, the luxury yacht was a clear step up in class from their current rickety vessel.

"Alright, that's what I'm talking about," Fernando said.

Greg slowed the boat and turned towards them. "Alright, here's the deal. When we get there, you all stay here until I speak to the owner. He was only expecting me and he gets a little jumpy."

"Anyone we know?" Tom asked.

"I doubt it," Greg replied. "Believe, me, it's better you don't know. Just wait here until I call you over."

Greg moved the boat to the stern of the yacht, which had a wooden diving deck attached. He idled the boat and pulled parallel to the deck, then hurried outside, tossing lines with his good hand to the men waiting on the other boat, who secured the rickety fishing boat to the infinitely more impressive vessel.

"Remember, wait here," Greg said, grabbing a bag from an overhead cupboard then climbed over the side onto the deck of the Lady of the Mist. Men dressed in black suits and dark sunglasses showed him onto the deck, where waiting for him was the man he had come to see, Victor Mallone.

"Greg, it's been a while my friend," he slobbered in his thick Italian accent.

"How are you, Victor? Well I hope?"

The near four hundred pound Italian limped towards Greg, leaning heavily on his cane. He had slick black hair heavy with grease, and although they were hidden behind sunglasses right now, cruel eyes befitting of his status as a gangland boss. Victor's most striking features however, were the network of scars that covered his face and in particular his arm. Nobody knew for sure how he got them, but Greg had heard the stories. Some said it was during the attack on his New York office by rival gangs, which had resulted in the death of his wife and family. Other rumours said it was a car bomb designed to kill him, which he had only survived because he had been too drunk to drive and had ordered one of his men to do it for him. There were even rumours that it was due to an altercation with Chinatown crime lord, Wang Li, who was said to have cannibalistic tendencies and had chosen Victor as a potential meal. No matter the reason, Victor wasn't a man you asked questions of, but one you answered. A dangerous man by any means, since his injuries, he had developed a ruthlessness and lack of compassion left by the death of those closest to him. The good thing about Victor for people like Greg was that if you had enough money and played by the rules, there was nothing that Victor couldn't or wouldn't get you. It had taken every penny Greg had, and whatever he could borrow from some of the Vegas loan sharks to get the money Victor had asked for. He only hoped now that the deal could be completed.

"You bring me my money?" Victor said in his Italian drawl.

"Of course," Greg replied, reaching into his jacket and handing over the bag he'd brought with him. "Fifteen grand as agreed."

Victor took the bag and handed it straight to one of his men, who disappeared into the boat.

"You're not even going to count it?"

"I know you wouldn't be stupid enough to short change me," Victor said, making Greg grateful the oversized Italians eyes were hidden behind his sunglasses.

"Of course not, this is business."

"Just so we're clear," Victor said, "you bring my boat back in one piece. Not a scratch, you hear me?"

"Of course."

"The equipment you asked for is in the cargo hold. This boat is special to me, it means a lot. I'd be upset if anything happened to it. You know what happens to people who upset me, don't you?" Victor said, giving Greg a crocodile smile.

Greg nodded. Everyone knew what happened if you crossed Victor.

"Okay, then I guess we have a deal," Victor said, then turned to one of his men, whispering something in his ear before the man promptly disappeared inside the vessel. Victor looked past Greg to Tom and his friends on the deck of his boat.

"Who are your friends?" the Italian asked.

"Assistants. They're helping me."

"They're just kids."

"They were cheap."

"You really think there's a monster out there?" Victor said, smiling at Greg.

"I'm sure of it."

"Well," he said with a shrug, "it's your money and time. Who am I to tell you that you're wasting it."

Remembering how volatile a man he was dealing with, Greg said nothing, preoccupied by the appearance of the two brutes that were approaching Victor from inside the boat. It was obvious they were related, they shared the same sharp blue eyes and hooked noses. Both had blond hair, the taller, stockier of the two, wore his in a buzz cut and had a light stubble. His leaner but no less intimidating sibling was clean shaven and wore his hair in a side parting. Both were wearing black combat trousers and boots with a T-Shirt tight enough to show off their muscular physiques.

"Ah, right on time," Victor said, grinning at Greg's discomfort. "These are the Russev brothers. The tall one here is Alexi. His English isn't so good but he knows enough to get by. This is his brother Pavel. You speak to him mostly, he knows English well."

"I don't understand," Greg replied, both confused and a little afraid of the most recent events.

"They are my insurance policy, chaperones if you will," Victor said, unleashing another sleazy grin.

"For what?"

"They will stay with you, assist you."

"This wasn't part of the deal, Victor. We had an agreement, I already have my assistants."

"You sound ungrateful," Victor said, the shift in his voice reminding Greg to be cautious.

"I'm sorry, I don't mean to be ungrateful, I just don't understand."

Greg glanced at the Russev brothers, who stared back with icy indifference.

"You don't think I would just turn my boat over to you and leave you to your own devices?" Victor chuckled.

"I, uh, I thought those were the terms of our agreement."

"It seems you misunderstood," the sleazy Italian said. "The Russev's will accompany you, to keep an eye on things, to make sure you don't put my beautiful boat at risk whilst you search for your monster. Besides, they can assist you with the cargo you requested and make sure it's handled safely."

"No disrespect, but I can handle it myself."

Victor stared at Greg's singular hand and grinned. "I don't agree. Besides which, this is non-negotiable."

Greg squirmed, which only seemed to increase Victor's enjoyment.

"Okay, maybe they can be of some use," Greg said, trying to ignore the butterflies in his stomach.

"Very good, I knew you would see things my way," Victor replied, clapping his hands together. "There is just one more thing."

"Go on."

"These men, the Russevs," Victor said as he patted the sweat from his forehead with a handkerchief, "they are good men. Some of the best. Very efficient, very much in demand. I'm afraid their services are going to cost an extra five thousand."

"But I didn't-" Greg stopped, sensing the dangerous shift in atmosphere. Both Victor and the Russev's were staring at him, and he thought that if he pushed much harder, he might find himself tied to the anchor and dropped overboard.

"Mr Mallone," Greg said, forcing himself to remain calm, "please try to understand, this offer, as generous as it was, is completely unexpected. I don't have the money to pay for this. I'm cleaned out."

Victor paused for a second, flicking his tongue against his top lip like some fat desert lizard. "Okay, I see the dilemma. Here's what I'm going to do. I'll give you the Russev's now on the understanding that you pay me when you bring my boat back. Because I consider you a friend, I'll only charge you interest at a thousand a day. I don't think I need to tell you what will happen if you don't pay up."

"No, I understand," Greg said, his stomach tightening as he was pushed further into a deal he had no means of honouring. "I appreciate it, thank you."

"What are friends for?" Victor beamed. "You go out now and

you find your fish. Your boat will be at Washington dock. When you return my boat and bring me my money, you will get it back, understood?"

Greg nodded.

II

Ten minutes later, Greg stood on the deck of the Lady of the Mist with Tom, Fernando, Jim Joanne and Marie watching his boat as it headed back to land, taking Victor and his men with it. He hoped he would feel better once the slobbering Italian was on his way, yet the noose around his neck, if anything, felt tighter. The Russev's had already headed below deck, and Greg was left with the problem of not only locating the creature, but also doing it as quickly as possible to avoid falling too far into debt with Victor.

"Okay," he said with a sigh, "let's get moving, shall we?"

"How will we know where to look?" Tom asked.

Greg grinned. "It will be easier than you think."

CHAPTER TWENTY

The Scottish highlands were being barraged by blustery winds and icy rain, which stung the skin. The rolling green grasses off the dirt path danced under its power as Rainwater trudged towards his destination. Squinting against the elements, he could see the house down the hill sitting on the edge of the water that was white tipped and violent as it slammed against the dock. He had arrived unannounced, and only hoped he had come to the right place.

The wind howled in his ears and rocked him on his heels, slapping his sodden jacket against him.

The house stood alone, a singular wooden property. Outside, there was a rusty red truck without wheels, propped up on bricks with its innards missing. There were also buckets of fishing line and mounds of what Rainwater could only call junk, piles of things that seemed to have little in the way of practical use. A set of old car tyres, dozens of rusty steel containers piled haphazardly, and stacks of wood pallets stacked by the house, which for all intents and purposes looked uninhabited. Rainwater walked towards the door, every bit as cold, wet, and miserable, as the weather, and half wondering what he would do if the person he was looking for wasn't home, didn't live there any more, or was even still alive.

He knocked on the door and waited, praying someone would answer. He hadn't had a drink since he left America, and his addiction was screaming at him for attention. He knocked again, and cupped his hands to look through the grimy windows, only able to see shadowy husks of furniture within.

"Can ae help ye?"

Caught by surprise, Rainwater spun around to face the man who was walking towards him from the water's edge. He was wearing a tattered green parka and red baseball cap. In one hand, he was carrying a fishing rod, in the other, two magnificent trout with their skin glistening in the rain.

"I'm looking for someone," Rainwater said as the man stopped in front of him.

"Who ye after?" the man said, his Scottish accent thick and difficult for Rainwater to understand.

"Ross Mackay. I was told he lived here."

The man nodded, his eyes shining behind the shadow of his hat. "You a yank?"

"Excuse me?"

"Yank. Are ye one?"

"Uh yeah. I'm American," Rainwater said.

"You from the Government?"

"No."

"Then whataya after?"

"My name is Henry Rainwater, I was looking for-"

"Rainwater ye say?" The man said, showing a little interest.

"Yes."

The man nodded. "Aye, well, it looks like you found who you were tryin' to find."

"You're Ross Mackay?"

"Aye, that I am."

"You don't know me but I was-"

"You were pals with me brother."

Rainwater nodded, running a hand through his rain sodden hair. "That's right. He saved my life."

"Still dead though."

"Yes, I'm afraid so."

"So whaddya want with me?"

Rainwater looked around the isolated landscape. "I just wanted to get away from my old life and start fresh. Just before he died, your brother told me I should come here if I felt like I needed to leave my past behind."

"Were ye with him, on the boat when it wen' down?"

"Your brother didn't die at sea," Rainwater said. "I know that's what the government told you, but it's not how it went down."

Ross didn't look in the least bit surprised, then strode past Rainwater handing him the fish as he approached the door. "Ye better come in then and fill me in. We'll see what happens after that dependin' on what ye have tae tell me."

II

Rainwater followed Ross into the cabin, glad to be out of the rain. His host shrugged off his jacket and hung it on one of the pegs by the door, did the same with his hat half turned to Rainwater. "Ye can put the fish in the kitchen, and then hang yer coat up. Ah don't want ye drippin' water all over mah floors."

Rainwater nodded and looked around the open plan space. It was filled with the clutter of a single man. The entire back wall of the room was an enormous bookcase filled with dusty leather bound books alongside the more modern, glossy literature. Through an open door, Rainwater could see the foot of an iron bedstead, through another the white edge of a bath. To his right the living area was small but inviting, and dominated by a stone fireplace and what looked like a regularly used log fire. To his left was the only other door, which Rainwater presumed must be the kitchen. Ross was on his knees in front of the fireplace loading logs into the hearth, for the time being, completely ignoring his houseguest. Rainwater pushed open the door, relieved to see that he was right, and the kitchen lay beyond. Like the rest of the house, it was simple in its decor. Tired wood table, old-fashioned cupboards around the outer edge, and on the far wall, a white cooker that looked like it was from the seventies, a white double fridge freezer and washing machine.

Rainwater put the fish in the sink and took another look around the dingy room, his eyes locking onto the bottle of Famous Grouse whisky on the countertop. His guts ached to taste it, but Rainwater knew that it wouldn't help his cause if he were to help himself to his hosts booze before they had even settled down to talk. Forcing his addiction aside for the time being, he returned to the sitting room.

Ross had managed to light the fire, and it hissed and crackled as it devoured the wood. Rainwater slipped off his sodden jacket and hung it up as instructed.

"Sit yersel' doown," Ross said, motioning to the dog-eared chair by the fire as he took his own seat. Rainwater instead headed to the fireplace, warming his hands on the flames and trying to rid some of the chill from his bones. Ross waited for Rainwater to warm his hands and take his seat. In the glow of the fire, Rainwater couldn't help but be awed, without the heavy coat pulled up over his neck and the baseball cap covering his face, by how much Ross resembled his brother. They were almost identical.

"So," Ross said with a sigh as he grabbed a beaten tin of tobacco from the arm of the chair and began to roll a cigarette. "Tell me what happened with mae brother."

"Well, I take it the government gave you the sinking boat story."

"Aye, arse faced prick called up to the hoose tae tell me."

"Well, that's not what happened. You know about the accident on the Red Gold? The sinking?"

"Aye, I know it." Ross's expression changed. "You're him, you're that Harris kid."

"You know about me?"

"Oh aye, our Jimmy, told me all aboot you."

"Jimmy," Rainwater said wistfully, "I never knew him as that. He was always just Mackay to me."

"Sounds aboot right. He never did like his name. Didn't think it fit."

Rainwater nodded and stared into the fire, which was slowly starting to warm the room.

"So," Ross said, putting the cigarette in his mouth and lighting it, "about mah brother. What happened?"

Rainwater wasn't sure which laws he was actually breaking by disclosing what had actually happened to Mackay, and he cared even less. He relayed it all as best he could remember. When he was done, the fire was roaring in the hearth and the room was warm. Like his brother before him, Ross wasn't one to jump in or interrupt. Instead, he listened without comment. Rainwater finished, feeling infinitely better for getting this particular monkey off his back. He waited for a reaction from Ross, who was watching him, flames reflecting in his eyes from the fire.

"Alright," he said, tossing the end of his cigarette into the flames.

"That's all you have to say? Don't you have questions or anything?"

"Nope. Ye answered all mah questions."

Rainwater stammered, and shifted in his seat.

"Wassamater wi ye?"

"Nothing, I just... I thought you might have more to say, that's all."

"Nothin else te say."

"So you believe me?"

"Aye. It sounds more like oor Jimmy the way ye describe it. Better than the fookin' shite story I was given first time roond anyway. As fer yer sea monster, well,
I'll keep mae opinions tae masel'."

"Okay, I respect that."

"So, wi that outa tha way, what is it ye really want?"

Rainwater cleared his throat, unsure if he even really knew the answer to the question. "Well, I was hoping to stay here for a while, clear my head. I'm willing to work of course, whatever it takes to earn my keep."

"I'm not so sure aboot that. As ye might ae noticed, this place ain't exactly welcomin'.There's a reason it's oot ere in tha middle o' nowhere. I like mah privacy. Ah don't like to be bothered."

"I won't get in your way. I just need a quiet place away from the world to get my head together. Somewhere off the grid, somewhere I can stay hidden if I want to. Somewhere like this."

Ross didn't answer. Instead, he opened his tobacco tin and started to roll another cigarette. "Our Jimmy sais you were a fisherman once, before all this monster talk. Are ye willing to go oot on the water?"

Rainwater looked out of the window at the churning, white tipped waters of the lock. "Yeah, I fish."

"Ah know ye fish. Ahm askin' if yer willin to go oot there?"

"What do you catch?"

"Trout or salmon. None o' those king crabs mah brother used to fish in the Bering sea. Mug's game that. Dangerous stuff."

"The lock," Rainwater said, trying to choose his words carefully, "is it...landlocked?"

"Aye, it is. Don't worry, lad, yer monster won't find ye here. Oor Nessie might though, eh?" Ross said with a smile.

"So I can stay then?"

"As long as ye earn yer keep, and only because yer a pal of oor Jimmy, else ye'd be doown the road."

"Thank you, I really appreciate it."

"Aye well, let's just see hoow it all works oot. Ahm not used to havin people aroond."

"As I said, I'll keep out of your way."

"Ye'll ave tae kip on the sofa. Only got one bed."

"That's fine. I don't mind."

"Alright then. Ye start earning ye keep in the morn. Up at half past five. I wanna be oot on the water by six."

"Understood. I'll be ready."

"There's just one thing ah doont understan'," Ross said as he lit his cigarette. "Why oot here? Don ye have a lassie? Someone tae help ye get through whatever this is yer hidin' from?"

"No, not anymore. I did once. She was part of it too, the expedition to find the creature. She was with me when Mackay sacrificed himself to save us. Anyway, for a while after, we were together, we were helping each other to get through, and then, things changed."

"She cheat on ye?" Ross asked.

"No. She outgrew me. It was my fault. I was just too stupid to see it until it was too late."

"Aye, women'l do that te ye. Makes a man really see his limitations, eh lad?"

"Yeah, well, she made me see mine. I just didn't know how to deal with them."

"So where is she noow, this lassie o' yours?"

"I don't know," Rainwater said with a sigh, "I really have no idea."

CHAPTER TWENTY-ONE

Four thousand miles away, Clara Thompson sat on the deck of the boat, infinitely less excited than she expected to be. Her two camera operators, Toby and Luke, were rigging static cameras to the frame of the boat as they made their way through the north Atlantic. She stared at the water, trying to figure out exactly what went wrong with her life. The plan was to refuel in Brazil before making the journey south to the Antarctic waters where Clara had first encountered the creature's mother. She had no scientific reason for choosing such a route, it just seemed logical. Ideally, she would rather not be out there at all. The horrific memories of last time out were still fresh, and reminded her more than anything of just how much she had changed. Something caught her eye then, something unusual enough to snap her from her self-pity. The shadows on the deck were moving, shifting position. She looked out to sea, taking a second really to feel how the boat was moving. There was no doubt about it. They were turning around.

She stood, just about to head inside to question Andrews, when he arrived, striding onto the deck.

"We're heading back to Washington," he said before Clara could say anything.

"Why?"

"We had a carcass wash up on a beach in Madagascar. Definitely a victim of our creature."

"Madagascar? Are you sure?"

"My team reviewed the images and video footage. It's definitely our creature."

"It makes no sense, unless of course..." Clara frowned, for the first time really engaging the scientific portion of her brain. "The aquarium where you held the creature. What temperature was the water?"

"What does it matter?"

"Never mind why, just answer the question."

"Around seventeen degrees I think."

"Jesus Christ, didn't you think to tell me this before we set out?" Clara said.

"Well, I would have mentioned it if you weren't busy planning shots with your damn TV crew. What does it matter anyway?"

"It matters because it completely changes where we should be looking for this thing. When we encountered the first creature, it had acclimatised to living in colder Antarctic waters. Sure enough, it could go into warm water to feed, but always went back to the cold, to its preferred environment. I would have expected those conditions to be replicated when it was placed into the facility in Florida."

"We were going to, but Doctor Comwell thought it would be better to keep the creature in a more hospitable temperature."

"Why?"

"Well, if we needed to get in the water and repair the structure or clean the filters, it would be easier on the dive crews."

Clara shook her head. "So you're telling me you changed this creature's natural environment just to make sure your staff wouldn't get a chill if they had to go into the water?"

"It wasn't just that, it was the costs. We couldn't afford the modifications needed to keep the water cold enough."

"I'm not sure I believe that, but either way, it changes everything. By keeping the water temperature higher, the creature has obviously adapted to the new environment. The aquarium was in essence its comfort zone. It's all the creature ever knew. Now it's out there in the world, my best guess is it will be looking to replicate the conditions of the holding tank as best it can."

"You think Madagascar is the right place for that?"

"Could be. The Indian Ocean is rife with underwater caves. Most of them are deep and isolated. Potentially it's the perfect place for our creature to call home."

"But we don't know for sure?"

"No, but the conditions are right, and if there's a kill on the beach, it's a hell of a place to start looking."

"That's why we're going back. We'll never get there on a boat this size. Tomlinson has a plane waiting to take us to the kill. We can hire a boat when we get there."

Clara nodded. The flash of excitement had reminded her of the life she had left behind, a time when things seemed much simpler.

A time before you became a fraud.

Her inner voice was, of course right. Behind the hard exterior, she was incredibly fragile. Worse than that she was completely alone. She had sacrificed her life for a career, and even that was built on a lie. She thought about Rainwater, and wondered if the reason for his self-destruction was because he was feeling the same way. Despite the gulf which had grown between them, they were actually more alike than she was comfortable with admitting.

Something inside her, a feeling deep down in her gut told her she was heading into dangerous territory, not just with Andrews, but by pursuing this creature for the second time. Her mother always used to tell her not to push her luck too far, because eventually, you were bound to lose. Clara thought this was one of those situations, and the only outcome would likely be bad.

II

After a two hour boat ride back to Washington, a twenty hour flight to Madagascar and another three hours out at sea on their much larger and more luxurious boat, Clara and the rest of the crew were exhausted. She had tried to sleep on the flight, yet despite the luxury afforded by the private jet sent by the government, she couldn't settle. As exhausted as her body was, her mind raced and pondered on scenarios, about decisions made and ones yet to come to fruition. The result was she was running on empty, and even the beautiful blue skies of an equally beautiful day couldn't lift her spirits.

Andrews sat opposite her in the luxury lounge area on the inside of the hundred and forty foot luxury yacht. "So, where are we heading?" he said, rolling out a chart on the table.

"The cave system beneath us is pretty extensive. There are so many places it could be hidden that our best chance is to cover as much area as possible, depending on the fuel we have."

"Don't worry about the fuel. This boat can do almost seven thousand miles on a single tank."

"Are you sure about that? It seems like a lot."

"Absolutely. As much as people hate the government, we do

get some perks," Andrews said, trying to lift Clara's spirits.

Despite herself, she returned his smile and relaxed a little. "Alright, I'll take you at your word. Now you say the tracker on the creature has a range of around five miles, right?"

"Yeah."

"Okay, here, take a look at this." She placed a plastic overlay onto the map, and started to draw a series of lines on it in red pen. "These are the migratory patterns of orcas and blue whales at this time of year. It stands to reason that our creature would be targeting these as a food source."

"Wouldn't we have seen remains washing up, or whales beaching themselves like last time?"

"No. Remember, the creature then was enormous. At over three hundred feet, it was natural to expect it to cause panic amongst the local wildlife. Although big, the current creature isn't large enough yet to cause that level of agitation. As for remains, again, we need to consider the size of the creature. Unlike before, where everything was a potential meal, the creature won't attack anything too large. Things like blue whales for example would be too risky. It will stick to smaller prey, things around half its size. The downside to that is that anything it kills and doesn't finish off will be devoured by other sea predators before it ever makes landfall."

"Okay, so what do we do to find this thing?"

"Can you get choppers out here?" She asked.

"No problem. Whatever you need."

"We need some in the air spotting the whales as they migrate. They will be able to see any attack by our creature way before it comes and give us an idea of where we ought to be."

"Okay, yeah, of course, that's a great idea," Andrews said, genuinely impressed. "How will they know what to look for?"

"They'll know when they see it. It might be an idea if I go up there too. I can probably do more up there than down here anyway."

"Alright, I'll make a few calls, see what I can do. In the meantime, can I give you a little advice?"

"As long as it's not to get some sleep. If it is, I've tried," she replied with a smile.

"Try harder. You look like you could use it. You won't do anybody any favours, yourself included if you burn out. There's a long way to go yet."

"You're right. The problem is, I *can't* sleep. I've tried. My damn mind won't rest."

"Can I make a suggestion?" Andrews said.

"Go ahead."

"Go back to this Clara," he said as he rapped on the map with his knuckles. "Leave that one behind," he added, nodding to the camera crew who were filming their conversation.

"You know I can't do that. There are expectations on me, I have commitments."

"To who? Your readers? Your agent? Rainwater? What about you? Where do you find the time to do what you want to do?"

"I have no regrets," she snapped, "I'm happy in my new life."

"Then answer me one thing."

"Go on."

"Why is it that in all the time since we first set off from Washington, the happiest I've seen you is just then when you were drawing on that map?"

She opened her mouth, but no words came. Instead, she closed it and waited for Andrews to go on.

"Russo picked you for a reason. Hell, *I* picked you for a reason. You were the best. For the record, I think you still are if you can get your head out of your ass and remember who you used to be."

"What's so wrong with trying to make something of myself?"

"Nothing at all as long as it's what you actually want."

"It is."

"Well, in that case, I'll shut up about it. Either way, try to get some rest. I'll go make those calls."

CHAPTER TWENTY-TWO

Greg stood in the cargo hold of the Lady of the Mist, looking at the equipment spread out in front of him. Pavel, the shorter of the two Russev brothers and the only one who seemed to have any grasp of the English language, stood beside him.

"You understand equipment, yes?" he said flatly.

"Yeah, I understand it. It's a tracker of some kind."

"Yes. Long range, very expensive," Pavel said, turning his icy gaze on Greg.

"Believe me, I know how expensive it was. It's costing me a fortune. Where's your brother?"

"He drive boat."

"Good. Are you sure this will work?"

"Yes. American government are stupid. They scramble signals and think they stay hidden when scrambled signal itself is just as easy to trace."

"So where they go, we follow?"

"Exactly," Pavel said.

"How will we know which signal is theirs?"

"Government use very specific frequency, very unique."

"Okay then, let's get to it. I need to get on with this as quickly as possible. Is the other cargo secure?"

"Yes. It's in the back there," Pavel said, nodding towards the crate in the corner.

The Russian started to assemble the tracker as Greg walked across the hold, laying his hand on the hip high wooden box. Inside, was his vengeance, one that he hoped to take soon.

II

Twenty minutes later, the scanning equipment had been set up. Pavel was sitting at the desk in front of the unit, which resembled an old radio with a dial on the front. The unit was attached to a computer, and the Russian was frowning, one ear pressed to the headphones whilst he turned the dial with the other.

"I think I find signal," he said, making a few minor adjustments to the controls. Greg hurried to the desk, hoping to see something he understood instead of a computer screen full of numbers.

"What am I looking at here?"

"Scrambled data. Definitely government signal."

"Where?" Greg asked.

"Wait," Pavel said as he made a minor adjustment to the dial, then turned to the keyboard and started to punch in commands. "This is Russian technology. If the Americans knew we had this, it would cause all sorts of trouble, you understand?"

"I thought the cold war was over," Greg said, trying to keep the tone light.

"You think we stop watching just because countries no longer fight?" Pavel said, flashing a white grin at Greg. "You people are more ignorant than I thought."

"I don't care about squabbles between countries. For the record, I'm an Australian, not a yank."

"I know. Otherwise, we wouldn't be showing you this equipment."

"So how do we find out where the signal is?" Greg said, trying to get the conversation back on track.

"Within scrambled signal sent by Americans is GPS data. All boats have to have this to enable radar to function. The Americans think signal is hidden and untraceable. This system reverse engineers signal and lets us trace."

"So, can we set it off and find out where we need to go?"

"Already doing it. It takes a little time to unlock information. It shouldn't take long," Pavel said as he entered more commands onto the computer screen. "Here, I think we have it."

Pavel clicked a button on the screen, and the jumble of numbers switched to a world map. "There," he said, zooming in on the red marker on screen. "Indian ocean, just off coast of Madagascar."

"Jeez, that's miles away from where we are."

"A few days, yes."

"Will we have enough fuel?"

"Yes. This vessel designed for long distance. Fuel won't be a problem."

Greg watched as Pavel scrawled down coordinates onto his notepad.

"I'll give the data to my brother. In a few days, we will be right on top of them."

Greg nodded, glancing back towards the crate in the corner, then down at the fleshy stump of his wrist, realising that soon, the last few years of hell would finally be avenged, no matter the cost to anyone else.

CHAPTER TWENTY-THREE

The charcoal grey helicopter sliced through the air, keeping pace with the pod of twelve sperm whales as they moved through the crystal clear waters below. Ever since the banning of all whaling in the area, the Indian Ocean had become something of a sanctuary for the majestic animals.

Clara watched through binoculars as the creatures obliviously went on their way, occasionally breaking the surface to breathe. For the last three days, she had tracked more than five separate pods, all without any sight of the creature. She had expected to see something, perhaps diversionary tactics to avoid an encounter, and yet, there was nothing to report. The radio on her lap crackled, and she picked it up.

"This is Thompson."

"You see anything out there?" Andrews said, his voice distorted by static.

"I'm still tracking this pod of sperm whales."

"It's been three days now. I would have expected to see something by now."

"Look, this isn't an exact science. I'm doing my best."

"Just keep in mind, the batteries on the tracker probably only have a week or so left before they die. We need to do this now."

"A week? How did you change them back in the aquarium?"

"It wasn't so hard. We had a harpoon that fired a small micro tracker. It was more than adequate."

"You didn't remove the old one?"

"There didn't seem to be any need. We just implanted a replacement once the batteries had died."

"That's inhuman, and cruel."

"Look, we can talk about the morals of the past later. Can we please just get on with things for now?"

"I hear you. We'll need to head back in soon to refuel anyway. I'll meet you back at the dock."

"Copy that," Andrews said, and clicked off. Clara set the radio back on her knees and lifted the binoculars, finding the whales again.

She was about to ask the pilot how much fuel they had left when the whales veered off to the right and increased their speed.

Heart hammering in her chest, she lowered the binoculars and looked out of the domed glass of the helicopter, squinting against the sun. She could see no visible disturbance, nothing that would explain the sudden deviation. With her throat suddenly dry, she returned to the binoculars to get a closer look. The whales were obviously in a hurry, their previous leisurely progress replaced with an urgency, which was plain to see. She watched as the adults moved to the outside, sheltering the calves in the middle of the pod. She had seen this behaviour before. It was a classic defence mechanism against a potential predator.

Without looking away, she reached down and picked up the radio, lifting it to her mouth.

"Andrews, you there?"

She waited, listening to the static and watching the whales.

"Yeah, I'm here. What's happening?"

"Something's going on with these whales. They just veered off course and went into defensive formation."

"Is it the creature?"

"Maybe, it could just as easily be another predator. I'm tracking them now. Do you have our location?"

"Got you on GPS. We're around ten miles out."

Start heading this way, just in case we're on the money. If this thing is nearby, the tracker should be readable easily enough."

"Got it, I'm on my way. Keep me posted."

Clara returned her attention to the Whales, watching the surrounding water for any disturbance. She turned to the pilot. "Can we get any lower? The glare of the sun is making it hard to see."

The pilot gave the thumbs up, and dropped to within two hundred feet of the water. Able to see better, she lowered the binoculars and scanned the water, searching for whatever was hunting the whales. She turned her attention back the giant mammals as they swam on at pace. Her heart froze for a second, and then began to beat at double tempo.

One of the whales was missing. Of the twelve she had been tracking, there were now only five adults', three juveniles, and three calves. She counted again, forcing herself to take her time and ensure she didn't miss any. There was no doubt. One of the calves was gone. She craned her neck, scanning the surrounding water, wondering if it had grown tired and been left behind. For miles in every direction, all she could see was the calm ocean. She turned back to the pod, just in time to see a second calf dragged under.

"Jesus, did you see that?" She said to the pilot, who either didn't hear or chose not to answer. She estimated that the calf was around eight feet long, and had been dragged under by something that was obviously much larger, something she still couldn't see due to the glare on the surface. She snatched up the radio.

"Andrews?"

"Yeah, I'm here," he replied almost instantly.

"I think we've found it."

"Visual confirmation?"

"No, not yet. Too much surface glare. Something just dragged two whale calves under though, and I can't think of anything other than our creature that would be able to do that."

"We're inbound, will be there as soon as we can."

"Hurry up. I'm not sure how long it will feed."

"Got it, we're at full speed."

"Roger that," she said, only half listening.

She stared at the water, her mind playing tricks on her. Through the glare, she imagined she could see it, slivers of movement under the waves. All she could do now was keep track of the whales and hope Andrews would arrive in time.

II

Andrews increased speed, pushing the boat towards Clara's location. He checked her position on the GPS and adjusted his course, making sure he stayed with her as she tracked the whales. He glanced at the tracker, which was set up on the instrument panel, hoping to see the screen flicker to life as they locked onto the signal from the creature. He was within range now, with less than five miles between him and Clara. If she was right, he should be seeing a signal anytime soon. The boat bounced over a particularly choppy series of waves, electing a grunt from Clara's camera crew who were playing cards at the table.

He could see her helicopter now in the distance, a black speck on the horizon. He made a slight adjustment, vaulting over another wave and slamming the bow of the boat into the water hard enough to send a great wall of spray into the air. It was then that Andrews heard it, a steady and monotonous beeping sound. Glancing at the tracker, he couldn't help but smile as he saw the green sound wave on the screen. He snatched the radio out of its housing, grinning like a Cheshire cat.

"Clara, come in."

He waited for what felt like an eternity for a response. "Go ahead."

"I owe you a drink. I have a signal, repeat, I have a signal. Do you have visual confirmation yet?"

"Not yet. This damn glare is making it impossible. "

"Okay, standby, you should be able to see me coming in."

"Yeah, got eyes on you now. Come in steady."

"Why? You afraid I might spook the whales?" Andrews said.

"No, I'm worried our creature might decide you're its dessert," she fired back.

"Thanks," Andrews grumbled.

"Do you have a strong enough signal to track it now?"

"Yeah, no problem."

"Alright, in that case I'm coming back to the boat."

"Don't you mean to the dock?"

"No, I mean the boat."

"How the hell do you expect to get from the helicopter to here? Swim?"

"Not exactly."

"Then what?"

"Tell the crew to get the cameras ready and stand by on deck."

CHAPTER TWENTY-FOUR

Tom stood at the rear of the Lady of the Mist, looking out at the ocean. He could no longer see land in any direction, which increased his feeling of complete isolation. Three days had passed at sea, and with each one, the tension seemed to increase. Joanne was acting strangely, and had withdrawn into herself almost as much as Marie had. Jim and Fernando were also subdued, although he thought that could be due to how intimidating the Russev brothers were. On more than one occasion, Tom had tried to make conversation with Pavel and was greeted with monotone answers and an icy stare.

He got the impression that their presence wasn't exactly welcomed by Greg either, who spent his hours skulking about the ship as they headed towards Madagascar. He looked like a man who had the weight of the world on his shoulders, and wasn't quite sure how to deal with it.

"Peaceful out here, isn't it?"

Startled, and slightly spooked by the way that Greg had appeared as he was thinking about him, Tom nodded.

"Yeah, it's nice," he said as Greg joined him at the stern, looking out at the frothy wake thrown out by the boat, as it inched towards its destination.

"You know, this used to be my life, spending my time out here, before this," Greg said, raising his stump. "Those are years I'll never get back."

"It's not the end of the world you know," Tom said. "With prosthetics you can-"

"It's not the injury."

"Then what is it?"

Greg didn't answer immediately. Instead, he sighed and looked at the sun as it crept towards the horizon line, casting the ocean into glorious reds and oranges. "The guy's name was Paul Milla."

"Who?"

"The guy who died back when I last encountered this monster."

"From what you said at the motel, it was an accident. There's no way you could have known," Tom said.

"No, I get that. I've been diving, or at least I had been for more than ten years before that day. I thought I knew the ocean. I took it for granted until that thing swam out of the dark and changed my life forever."

Tom didn't answer. He didn't feel it was appropriate. Instead, he waited until Greg was ready to go on.

"You know what the worst part of it was?" Greg said, turning towards Tom.

"Go on."

"When we were down there, when I was pinned to the top of the cage with my air tanks running low, I wanted that man to die so I could save my own skin. I remember seeing him on the floor of the cage, hoping to see the air bubbles stop coming from his regulator so I could take it for myself. Even when I'd cut myself free, even through the fire that burned through my arm, I still considered leaving him for dead. I think I would have too if not for needing his wife to help get the cage out of the water. It wasn't until we were on deck and he'd actually died that I started to feel guilty about it."

"So why are you doing this? Why are you out here and risking putting yourself back in front of this thing?"

"I could give you a million answers you would expect me to give. Revenge. Closure. The truth is, I really don't know. All I can tell you is it's burning me up inside, and has been eating away at me ever since."

"Have you tried to talk to someone? Therapy maybe?"

"No. I knew by the looks on people's faces when I told them what happened that they didn't believe me. I'll never forget the surgeon who was looking after me post op for my arm. He seemed like a nice guy, a straight shooter. So he asks me what happened. Hell, maybe his colleagues put him up to it, I don't know, but as I said, he seemed sincere, so I told him all about the creature, all about what it did to the sharks. You know what happened?"

"What?"

"He laughed at me. Right there in my face. Man, I wanted to kill that prick. Would have done it too if I had the strength. Even now when I feel like giving up and letting this whole thing slide, I think about the way he laughed at me. This fish ruined me; that much is true, but I was the one who let it. This is my chance for a little payback."

"So why do you need us?"

Greg held up his amputated limb. "As stubborn a bastard as I am, there's only so much I can do without help."

"I don't get it," Tom said. "Isn't that why those Russian's are here?"

Greg grimaced, and glanced over his shoulder. "Let's just say they weren't supposed to be part of the deal."

"Can I ask you something?"

"Yeah, go ahead."

"That night you came to the motel. You didn't have someone outside watching us did you?"

"No, of course not. I had to tell you that though so you'd help me. I know you saw this monster, but trust me, that's just a baby compared to one that's fully grown."

"It was big enough."

"The point is, it's not even half its full length. You have a responsibility to put it right."

"This isn't my fault," Tom snapped.

"Bullshit it isn't. Like it or not, you and those friends of yours set it free. Are you telling me you won't feel guilty when it starts chewing people up whenever they decide to go in the water? I saw this thing cut through a whole army of sharks like they were nothing. I feel guilty over the death of just one man. Do you really think you can handle the guilt of the death of hundreds? Maybe thousands?"

"Thousands? Come on, that's a bit dramatic. It's just a fish," Tom mumbled.

"Just a fish? What happens when this fish destroys local fishing populations and disrupts migratory patterns of countless species? What about when fishing grounds used for years are suddenly barren because your fish has driven them away? What about people who rely on those fish to survive and make a living? True enough, maybe you won't see that death like you would like when they show the footage of wars and disasters on TV, but you would be responsible all the same. Believe me, you might not think so now, but you might just eventually thank me for dragging you out here."

"That all depends if we survive the trip," Tom muttered.

Inside the boat, Jim watched Greg and Tom in conversation, trying to keep control of his anger and paranoia, which were bubbling under the surface. Fernando joined him, sipping a bottle of water.

"How you doing, Jim?" he asked.

"What do you suppose they're talking about out there?"

"Small talk probably. My brother could talk the ears off a donkey."

"What if it's about us?"

Fernando glanced at his friend, frowning as he took another sip of water. "You okay, man?"

"Why would they just go out there on their own?" Jim said, ignoring the question.

From the table, Joanne looked at them, her stomach plunging into her shoes. Jim was using the same voice he had threatened her with back at the motel. Her eyes shifted to the knife on the table beside the plate of food she had barely touched.

"You sound paranoid," Fernando said, breaking into a nervous grin.

"Why shouldn't I be?" Jim said, glaring at Fernando. "We should have run when we had the chance. Now we're stuck here on this damn boat."

"Look, I don't think this guy intends to hurt us."

"What about them?" Jim said, rolling his eyes.

"The Russians?"

"Yeah."

"What about them?"

"Look at them. Shit, did you see the guy who they work for? The one who owns the boat? Don't tell me you didn't think he was a shifty guy. He looked like someone who would kill a man and not lose any sleep over it.

Just like me.

He almost added it, but cleared his throat instead as he stared out onto the deck at Greg and Tom.

"Hey, what's wrong with you?" Fernando said, frowning at Jim. "Where the hell did all this come from?"

Realising he'd gone too far, Jim forced a shrug and a grin which felt elastic on his face, as if his skin was loose and hiding the real him underneath. "I don't know, just stressed I suppose. Forget about it."

"Just relax," Fernando said, clapping Jim on the shoulder. "This will all be over soon enough."

Jim nodded and walked with Fernando back to the table to sit with the girls. Neither of them noticed that the fork from Joanne's plate was missing. As the two slid into the booth, Pavel came up from below deck.

"Where is Australian?" he said, giving them all a cold stare.

"Outside," Fernando said, pointing to the glass door leading onto the rear deck.

"Spasibo," Pavel said as he strode across deck and slid the door aside. Tom and Greg turned as one.

"We have a signal. Time to get device ready," he said.

Greg felt the tempo of his heart increase in anticipation. "Alright, let's do this," he said, following Pavel inside. "Come on, you two," he called over his shoulder, "and bring those two mates of yours."

CHAPTER TWENTY-FIVE

With the camera crew pointing at the helicopter as it approached and Andrews idling the boat, they watched as the chopper came in low, hovering just twelve feet above the deck. The rear door of the helicopter slid open, and Clara stepped out, one foot wedged in the winch hook. She was lowered down, making a show of it as she neared to the deck. She stepped off and waved the chopper away, waiting until the winch cable was retrieved and the helicopter was streaking away from them towards land.

"I thought you were making a documentary, not an action movie," Andrews grumbled as she joined him in the wheelhouse.

"Any movement?" She asked as she shrugged out of her jacket and tossed it on the table.

"No, the creature seems to be sticking to this area. It chased the whales for a while and then stopped, turning back and hanging around this location. It's gone deep now and doesn't seem to be moving."

"Hang on," she said, grabbing a sea chart and rolling it out on the table. "According to this, we're right on top of a pretty extensive cave system. It all seems to make sense."

"You think that's why it abandoned the whales? Because it didn't want to move out of its territory?"

"Usually that's not the case with predators. It's incredibly rare for them to abandon a kill."

"So why did it?"

"It's probably not as complicated as you think. Most species aren't as complex as humans are. It could just be that it had eaten its fill."

"Alright," Andrews said, reaching for his phone, "that's good enough for me."

"What are you doing?"

"Calling it in. Our job was to find this thing, nothing more. There is a destroyer and a sub waiting for our call."

"But you can't be sure this is our creature," Clara blurted.

"I thought you said I could."

"It's likely, but we really need visual confirmation."

"So what do you suggest, we wait until it surfaces?"

"No, that won't do it. If it has recently eaten it could be down there for a while."

"Well, it's a risk I'm willing to take. That's our tracking signal, so I don't think you need to worry. It's time to call our boys in to blow this thing out of the water."

"Explosives?"

"What else?"

"High powered stuff I take it?"

"Yeah, why."

"This entire cave system sits on a fault line. It's highly unstable. I wouldn't use anything explosive down there if I were you. You don't know what the outcome will be."

"Outcome? As long as the creature is dead, I don't care."

"If you detonate explosives down there, you could cause all kinds of seismic activity; maybe even trigger a tsunami if you bring those caves down. The structures are huge down there."

"Alright, so what do you suggest? We have the signal, it's obvious this is our creature."

"Just because you located the signal doesn't mean it's the creature," Clara said.

"Come again?"

"There are a number of reasons why we could have followed this signal here, and it could be something else."

"Come on, that's a stretch even for you," Andrews said. "Let's cut the crap, I know what this is really about."

"I have no idea what you mean," Clara said, looking anywhere but at Andrews.

"You came out here expecting to make some action packed documentary and are pissed because we accomplished our mission without drama."

"That's not it; I just want to be sure."

"Well, I'm sure enough. Give me one example of how this isn't our creature and I'll hear you out."

"Okay, let's say it got into a fight with some other predator, maybe a pod of aggressive orcas. It's possible one of them could have bitten the creature and took the tracker with it. Am I right in thinking the tracking device was close to the upper layer of the skin?"

"Yeah, it was," Andrews said, seeming less sure of himself.

"Well, doesn't that stand to reason as a possibility?"

"Possibly true, but unlikely," Andrews countered.

"Still, I can't imagine Tomlinson being too pleased if you drag that destroyer all the way out here and it is a false alarm."

Andrews grunted and paced the cabin, arms clasped behind his back. "Alright, so what did you have in mind?"

"It' simple really. The water here is relatively shallow, I can dive down there and-"

"Absolutely not."

"You didn't hear me out."

"I don't need to hear you out, the answer is no. I won't have deaths on this mission if I can avoid it. Sorry."

"Look, this is the only way to be sure. I'll dive down there and take a camera. As soon as I get visual confirmation, I'll come right back up. No heroics."

"And in addition to this good deed you get some breath taking one of a kind video footage to help you in your career, right?" Andrews snapped.

"Look, I haven't hidden the reasons I came out here. Yes, I want to get research material for the new book, but I also want to help. You should give me more credit."

"You should think more like the Clara from five years ago. She'd have kicked your ass for even suggesting this."

"People change," she said, feeling the colour rush into her cheeks.

"Not always for the best."

"Look, say what you will. I'm going down there and you can't stop me. You have no authority over me," she said, striding to the steps leading to the galley and cabins below.

"This is insane," Andrews said, grabbing her by the arm, "did you forget what happened last time?"

"That was different!"

"How? It seems the same to me, I won't let you kill yourself. I promised Rainwater I'd keep you safe."

"He has no say in what I do!" She screamed, pulling her arm

free. "Nobody does. He's probably too damn drunk even to remember that conversation."

"Then why don't we ask him?" Andrews said, grabbing his phone and scrolling to Rainwaters number.

"I thought you didn't know where he was?"

"I always knew where he was going. He's in Scotland. I planted a tracker in his case when I went to his apartment."

She shook her head, face twisted into a scowl. "You people really are slimy pieces of shit."

"There's the Clara I know," Andrews shot back.

"I'm going to get changed into my wetsuit," she said, heading down the steps. "Tell Rainwater to keep the hell out of my business. You do the same."

Andrews dialled the number and waited, phone pressed to his ear. "Come on, Henry, pick up the damn phone."

II

Rainwaters phone pulsed on the table by his bed. Reaching past the half-finished bottle of scotch with a hand, which felt like it, belonged to somebody else, he picked it up and lifted it to his eyes, squinting to see the display. He knew it was Andrews, and grimaced. As drunk as he was, he was nowhere near wasted enough to deal with the government official, and ignored the call. Despite his best intentions to get clean, the lure of alcohol had followed him all the way to Scotland. His sobriety had lasted less than one full day, and he was already in Ross's bad books after failing to get up in time to go out fishing. Like a snowball rolling down a hill, the more mistakes he made, the bigger his problem became. He could almost feel his body starting to give up the fight. He was starting to feel lethargic and old. He stared again at the phone, ignoring the questions racing around his brain.

What if something was wrong?

What if Clara was in trouble?

What if Andrews was calling to tell him something terrible had happened?

No.

He wasn't equipped to deal with any of those things in any way. Not yet. His eyes lingered on the scotch, the golden liquid seeming to invite him in, and its taste sure to rid him of worry and doubt and send him to the hazy place where things didn't matter.

"Fuck you, Andrews," he muttered to himself.

Tossing the phone on the table, he snatched up the scotch and took a long drink.

III

Clad in a blue wetsuit, Clara walked towards the deck. "So what did he say?" she said as she prepped her camera.

"He didn't answer."

"Drunk probably."

"Please, just wait, this isn't safe."

"You've been bitching at me to be the Clara of old. This is exactly what she'd do."

"I'll restrain you if I have to."

She paused, flanked by her camera crew. "So you're prepared to put your hands on a member of the public? That's assault. I'll have witnesses."

Andrews noted that the entire incident was being filmed. He smiled and shook his head. "You bitch. You manipulated this. This is all part of the show."

She didn't deny it, and didn't have to. The arrogant half smile said it all. "I'm doing this no matter what you say. Now are you going to help me or not?"

"This is a mistake. I want that on record."

"It is."

"Then it looks like I don't have a choice," Andrews muttered.

"Glad you see things my way. Now come on, we don't have much time."

CHAPTER TWENTY-SIX

He knew the dream well. It came to him often, and even when he was drunk like now, it still played out with awful vividness. It always started in the ice cave deep inside the Ross Ice Shelf just after Russo's grenade had exploded. Always clear, always vivid.

Screams reverberated around the chamber.
Ice splintered.
Debris fell.

Searing agony in his chest and leg brought Rainwater's world back into focus as he tried to shake off the intense ringing in his ears. He surveyed the scene. There were bodies scattered in and around the water. Some were incomplete. From his vantage point, he could see a severed leg bobbing across the surface of the water. Clara was on all fours, coughing and wiping away the blood, which now matted her hair against her cheek. She had been lucky. Mito was face down on the ice, his dead eyes staring into the floor from the pulpy remains of his face. One bloody arm hung out of the mound of ice, which had landed on Russo.

Rainwater got to his feet. The air was filled with pained moans of the wounded and dying. Some of the more fortunate of Russo's men had been out of the blast zone and were now helping their colleagues to safety.

Through the ringing in his ears, he could just about hear Clara screaming. He followed her line of sight, past the ice that had buried Russo towards Mackay. He was sitting in the water, leaning against the stranded juvenile creature, which had escaped mostly unscathed from the blast.

Mackay's entire left side was a burnt, charred mass of flesh. He was holding his stomach, and Rainwater could see soggy entrails protruding from between his fingers. Rainwater knelt beside him, blinking away tears as he held his friends' free hand.

"Hang on, Mac, we'll get you some help, we..."

"Don't," he said, his voice calm and accepting, "it's done. I'm

finished."

"We can get you out of here, and get you to a hospital..."

"Come on, lad, look at me. We both know I'd never make it. Besides, I killed a man. At least this way I won't have to spend the rest of my years in a prison cell."

In reality, it was at this point when Russo had shot Rainwater in the shoulder, only for Mackay to tie his foot to the young creature. As Russo had struggled, Rainwater, Clara, and the mortally wounded Mackay, had shoved the creature back into the water, taking Russo with it. They knew they had to end it, to destroy the creature. He saw his dream self in a time before he was a slave to alcohol. As always in his dream, Clara looked at his wounded shoulder.

"How bad were you hit?" she asked, looking at the blood seeping through his fingertips, as he clutched his shoulder.

"It's not too bad."

"Can you move?"

"Yeah, we have a bigger problem though," he said as he nodded towards the T7 on the ground.

"Remote was damaged by the blast."

"Then forget it. We need to get out of here."

"I'll do it manually."

"You can't stay here," Clara said, staring through the blood, which covered her face. "Let it go, we need to get out of here."

"We made a commitment to end this, and that's exactly what we need to do."

"The plan was to remote detonate, which we can't do now. Let's forget it. You don't need to become a martyr."

"People are dead because of me. This is what I deserve."

"Don't give me that hero crap," she said, glaring at him. "I lost someone too. We won't do their memory any good if we stay here. There'll be another chance."

"There won't, they'll come in and take it if we leave now. We have to finish it. You know I'm right," he said, looking Clara in the eye.

"I'll do it," Mackay gurgled. "We all know I'm gonna die here anyway. Let me go out my own way."

Clara looked at Rainwater. They both knew Mackay was right.

"You know what to do?" Rainwater whispered, feeling nauseous at the idea of leaving Mackay.

"Aye, I know what to do. You two get out of here. Just get me out of this bloody water first. I can't feel my legs," he said, trying to smile but only managing a grimace.

Rainwater and Clara dragged him out onto the ice, propping him against a jutting natural ledge. The ground beneath him immediately turned red with blood, which ran towards the water's edge. Rainwater positioned the weapon, helping Mackay get comfortable with it.

"Aim for the roof," he said, choking back tears. "This whole thing should..."

"I get it," Mackay said, finding a smile. "Now get out of here, both of you."

Clara started to help Rainwater to his feet, when Mackay grabbed him and pulled him close, whispering in his ear.

This was when the dream always changed. When Mackay had whispered in his ear for real, he had told Rainwater that if things got too bad, he should go to his brother in Scotland. In his dreams however, it played out very differently.

The frightened eyed, bloody faced Mackay of his dream would look at him in disgust.

"Why did I waste my life for you? Look at you. Pathetic."

In his dream, he panicked, tears welling up in his eyes. "I'm sorry, I'll change!" he screamed.

"You can't change. You're a waste. A fuckin' waste."

"I'm sorry, I-"

"Here," Mackay had said, shoving the concussion weapon at Rainwater. "You might as well stay down here with me since you've wasted your life."

He screamed at himself not to, yet, it always went the same way. The dream version of himself lifted the weapon towards the roof of the cave and fired, bringing the entire thing down on top of them to the sound of Mackay's laughter.

Water.

He gasped, coughing and gagging as he was dragged back to consciousness. He blinked, for a moment sure it was Mackay standing at his bedside before realising it was Ross, empty bucket still in his hands.

"Get yer arse up. Phonecall for ye."

Rainwater sat up, looking at his sodden pillow and pushing his wet hair out of his face.

"What did you do to me?" he coughed.

"Loch water. Only sure way tae wake yer up. Hurry up. This yank seems keen to talk te ye."

II

Clara swung her legs over the edge of the boat, and was suddenly a lot less brave than she initially thought. For as innocent as the crystal blue waters appeared, she knew that somewhere below, their monster lurked. Despite what she had told Andrews, she was in no doubt as to what she was heading towards. She was helped into the water by her camera crew, unable to still the racing tempo of her heart. Although she was a keen diver, she was a few years out of practice and had never dived under circumstances as extreme as this. She knew that the slightest error, the slightest loss of concentration, could lead to disorientation, and in turn, her being lost in the caves, destined for a painful death as she waited for her air to run out.

Pushing such negative ideas aside, she gave the thumbs up, kicking to stay afloat as the underwater camera was lowered to her. She had hoped Andrews would come out to see her off, but he had retreated inside, probably watching the feed from her camera and showing his dissatisfaction at her decision by not making an appearance on deck.

Knowing that if she put it off any longer, she might lose her courage, she took a last look at the bobbing hull of the boat, and then descended into the solitude of the Indian Ocean.

III

Dripping wet and significantly sobered up by his soaking, Rainwater stumbled from his bedroom to the main room of the cabin, sitting down heavily in the chair by the phone and picking up the receiver.

"Is this you, Andrews?" he grunted.

"Who else? I tried to call but you didn't answer your phone."

"I know. That's because I didn't want to talk to you."

"Trust me, you want to hear this. It' about Clara."

His breath caught in his throat. "What's happened?"

"We found the creature's lair, or at least we think we did."

"Antarctica?"

"Indian Ocean. We think it's in a cave system a few miles off the coast of Madagascar."

"What about Clara. What has she done?" Rainwater said, feeling the goose bumps pop up on his arms.

"You have to understand, I tried to talk her out of it, I tried to talk to her, but she's stubborn."

"What has she done?" Rainwater said, struggling to control his temper.

"Just remember, I did everything I could to-"

"Just answer the question," Rainwater snapped.

"She's in the water. She wanted to dive down and get a visual confirmation."

For a few seconds, Rainwater couldn't respond. A million responses seemed to jam between brain and mouth. He stammered, swallowed, and stammered again.

"You still there?" Andrews said, his voice hollow and distant.

"Why the hell didn't you stop her?" Rainwater blurted.

"What could I do? She's too damn stubborn for her own good. She wouldn't listen."

"So you just let her go? I told you to protect her."

"You were given every opportunity to come out here yourself and do that, so don't you put this on me."

The truth of Andrews's words stung Rainwater enough to derail his frustration. "Are you monitoring her?"

"She has an underwater camera with her. I have a live feed here on deck."

Rainwater stood and paced as Ross looked on. "Keep on the

line. I want you to update me on everything that happens."

"I can go one better than that. Do you have a computer there?"

"I brought my laptop."

"Power it up. I'll patch you into the feed."

"How can you do that, you don't know where I am?"

"Northern tip of Scotland, around two miles from the coast. You're in a cabin owned by Ross Mackay, who, if our satellite information is accurate, is there in the room with you."

Unsure if he was more disgusted or impressed, Rainwater sneered, hoping Andrews could sense the expression. "You always knew where I was, didn't you? Where I was going?"

"Of course I did. It's my job. Don't take it personally."

"Yeah, well, your plan won't work. I have my laptop but no internet connection here."

"Don't worry about that, I'll connect you via satellite. Go ahead and set it up."

Rainwater set the phone on the desk and hurried to his room, grabbing his laptop bag. Returning to the desk, he powered up the computer, waiting as it clicked and whirred into life. He snatched up the phone whilst he waited.

"Okay, I'm booting up now. Do you need anything from me?"

"No, the satellite is already on you. When you get a request for remote access, accept it and I'll do the rest."

Rainwater did as he was told, watching as his pointer moved about the screen of its own accord. Moments later, a window opened showing the unmistakeable ocean, as Clara approached the huge cave system on the sandy ocean floor.

"Okay, I have it," Rainwater said. "Can you communicate with her?"

"One way. She has an earpiece in, so I can speak to her. Unfortunately, she can't respond."

"Andrews, please get her up safely."

"I'll do my best."

Rainwater and Ross watched the footage as Clara made her way closer to her destination.

IV

165

The isolation of the ocean had brought a sense of calm to Clara, despite the danger she was swimming towards. Below her, appearing out of the gloom was the cave, its rocky mouth one of hundreds, which littered the ocean floor. Like the maw of some sea dwelling leviathan, the cave yawned towards her, its edges riddled with corals. Small fish lazily drifted in and out of Clara's vision as she slow kicked towards the entrance. Flicking on her torch, she shone it into the darkness, wishing its beam penetrated deeper and threw back more of the recessed dark areas beyond.

"Easy, Clara," Andrews's voice said in her ear, making her reflexively bite down on her regulator in fear and surprised at how loud it was. "Just be careful."

Dammit, Andrews, shut up. She thought as she left the open space of the ocean for the darkness. Her torch was barely adequate, and visibility was poor.

Clara swam into the depths, swinging the torch beam from side to side. It was as she was swallowed by the darkness, she realised what was bothering her so much.

There were no fish inside. Nothing stirred within the cave, and she suddenly felt incredibly isolated and alone. Adjusting the camera in her free hand, she followed the contour of the wall as it went deeper. Something came out of the darkness, a flash of white caught in her torch beam. She turned both camera and torch towards the half decomposed sperm whale skeleton where it lay on the floor of the cave, tiny chunks of rotten flesh moving with the currents on its body, as dozens of scavenger fish feasted on the remains.

"Okay, that must prove it," Andrews said in her ear. "Get the hell out of there."

She half considered it, especially when she saw there were more bones littering the cave, large creatures in their own right, which had been pulverised by some immense force of nature that could only be the creature they were looking for. The reason she didn't leave was because of what she saw beyond the remains, which littered the floor of the cave.

There were around ten eggs as far as she could tell, the milky spheres each around eight feet in diameter. Beyond them, at the back of the cave, she could see the creature. It was unaware of her as it pushed out another egg accompanied by a bloody cloud of fluids.

"Get out of there. Do it now," Andrews hissed in her ear.

She agreed it was time to go, and yet, couldn't help but stay where she was, knowing she was capturing something remarkable on film. She adjusted the torch, its beam flashing against the creature, which turned its massive head in her direction and started to move towards her.

This time she did move. Knowing there was no way she could get anywhere close to the surface before the creature got to her, she looked for somewhere to hide, a small space where the creature couldn't access. Eight feet away there was a cut in the cave, no more than a crevasse really, but big enough for her to squeeze into. Guessing that the creature was attracted to the light, she dropped the torch and took the camera with her as she swam for the hole. Confused by the splitting signal, the creature hesitated, before moving towards the visual stimulus of the torch beam. Clara squeezed into the gap, wishing there was more room for her to back up out of reach, but the rough wall gave her little room to move. It was then that panic set in, when she realised she had backed herself into what was nothing more than an underground coffin of sorts. Even the camera was momentarily forgotten in her distress, as was the rambling tone of Andrews in her ear as he yelled at her to get out. She lifted the camera with trembling hands and pointed it out of her makeshift prison.

Andrews on board the ship, Rainwater and Ross in Scotland, and Clara saw the creature, and could only look on as it lost interest in the torch which lay on the ground, and turned its attention towards her.

CHAPTER TWENTY-SEVEN

Tom knew the device was a bomb. Greg hadn't said as much, but it was obvious. He, Fernando, and Jim, were helping the Russev's carry the heavy, cumbersome device out onto deck. Tom flicked his eyes towards Joanne and Marie, and saw that they too knew what it was. Greg pushed the boat on, flashing excited glances over his shoulder at the device. In the distance, they could see the white hull of Andrews's boat, unaware that there was somebody in the water. Tom was conscious of the fact that as bad as things were when they set out, they might be about to get a hell of a lot worse.

They set the device down on the deck. Encased in a steel frame, the blue bowl within was where Tom suspected the explosives were housed. As if reading his mind, Pavel spoke, his grin wide as he chewed his way through the English language.

"Very high explosive," he said, switching his gaze between Tom and Greg. "We drop device off back of boat above target, and boom." He clapped his hands together. "Target destroyed."

Tom glanced at his brother, and then nodded to Pavel, who was speaking to his brother in Russian as they lit cigarettes. Tom and Fernando retuned to the table where the girls sat, pale faced and afraid.

"You have to do something about this," Joanne whispered as they sat down.

"What the hell can I do about it?" Tom said. "These aren't just your average guys on the street. They're killers."

"If we don't do something and you help them drop that bomb in the water, no matter what's down there, you'll be an accessory. You'll go down with them."

"Don't be so dramatic," Jim grunted. "If anyone asks what happened, we just say they forced us."

"I wasn't talking to you," Joanne spat, her hand almost going to the knife concealed in her jacket.

"Look, everyone just relax," Fernando said, trying to keep the peace. "Tom, you need to talk to the Australian guy. Get him to see sense."

"Why me?"

"Because you're the oldest. Plus, he seems to like you."

"I might be the oldest, but I didn't want any of this. This is all on you." He looked at the others as he said it, not even sparing Joanne for her part in it.

"Come on, please just try," Fernando said.

"You really think anything I say can change his mind? Just to let you know, a guy who hires Russian gangsters and brings a huge bomb out to sea isn't going to be talked out of whatever he intends to do by the likes of me."

"You have to try," Marie said, her voice cracking. It had been so long since she had spoken to anyone that they had almost forgotten she had come along. Of them all, she seemed to be suffering the most. Her eyes were wide and frightened. Tom thought she would make the great subject for a painting, so tragic and hopeless was the look in her eye.

"Okay, I'll try it, just don't expect any miracles," Tom said as he got up from the table.

He walked over to Greg, alarmed at how much closer they were to the other boat. He tried to put his thoughts into some kind of order, to figure out what to say, when Greg beat him to it.

"Don't bother trying to talk me out of it," he said without taking his eyes from the window.

"What do you mean?" Tom stuttered, completely thrown off guard.

"I'm disabled, not deaf. You and your friends should learn to whisper more quietly."

"Look, I get that you have issues with this thing, but we don't. I know we were in the wrong by freeing the creature, but just look how things have gone since then. Gangsters? Bombs? Where does it end? What happens to us?"

"You made your decision to come out here. Whatever happens now, happens."

"That's alright for you to say. These are people's lives you're messing with."

Greg turned towards him then, his face a twisted mask of rage. "You don't think I've suffered? You don't think my life was ruined by this thing? I never thought I'd ever get a chance for revenge and nobody - not you, or those government pricks out there are going to stop me."

"Come on, you must see what this is. You'll go to jail. We'll *all* go to jail. Is that how you want to live the rest of your life? Locked up in some prison cell?"

"My life has been like living in prison ever since that thing took my hand. I don't care what happens, just as long as this fish is dead."

"What if we don't help? You need us."

Greg glanced at Tom and smiled. "No. Maybe before I knew the Russev's were coming along I did, but not now. For as much as I don't particularly care if you help or not, they might," he said, jabbing a thumb over his shoulder towards the Russevs who were out at the stern of the boat, smoking and chatting to each other. "Trust me; you don't want to get on their wrong side, especially with these good looking girls on board. Do you understand what I'm sayin to you?"

Tom nodded. He understood perfectly. There was no choice, no option but to let it play out to the bitter end, whatever that might be.

"Get those pals of yours ready out on deck, we're almost on top of them."

II

Andrews didn't see the boat bearing down on them at first. His attention was fully on the screen showing grainy footage of the creature as it approached Clara. So far, it hadn't attacked, but that didn't make him feel any better about it. Rather than fear, it was anger that he felt. Anger at the situation she had put him in. If she, as a civilian - a celebrity no less - was to come to any harm under his supervision, he didn't like to think about what that could mean for his future. He could hear the muffled ranting of Rainwater down the phone, which was on speaker and lying on the table beside the monitor. Andrews wasn't ready to speak to him yet, he had no answers to explain the images he knew Rainwater was watching. He half considered cutting the feed before anything happened, however, knew that if he did, Rainwater was likely to try to contact Tomlinson, which was something Andrews wanted to avoid at all costs.

It was at that point, as he was torn between what to do that he heard the whine of the approaching engine. At first, he thought it might be local Coast Guard, or even Tomlinson sending someone out to check on him, but he dismissed both ideas immediately. The white hulled pleasure cruiser, which bucked over the water towards him at speed, was obviously a private vessel, the sunlight shimmering off the hull making it hard to see who was on board and why they were in such a hurry. Something in the pit of his stomach - call it instinct or some other intuitive sense, sent alarm bells ringing. The approaching boat was too deliberate in its direction, and was obviously approaching with a sense of purpose. He glanced at the monitor screen, which showed the creature rubbing its huge snout against the gap in the rock where Clara was wedged.

It can smell her.

He wasn't sure if 'smell' was the right terminology, but he was certain it knew she was there. It would be able to feel the racing tempo of her heart beat, perhaps even 'taste' the unusual scent of her in its domain. The shampoo on her hair, the makeup on her face - all things that were in the water and completely alien to the creature. As Andrews watched, a probing tentacle tip came into view, pushing gently against the gap in the rock face.

"You," Andrews said to one of the cameramen, whose name he couldn't remember, "watch that monitor. Let me know if anything happens."

"Clara said I'm to keep filming the surface in-"

"I'm in charge here," Andrews raged. "In case you haven't noticed, she's in danger. Forget recording, this is a person's life we're talking about."

The cameraman nodded, hurrying to the monitor beside Andrews, who in turn went out on deck, grabbing the binoculars from a hook by the door. He focussed on the approaching boat, his stomach filling with ice.

At the stern, four men were lifting a silver framed object onto the transom. Andrews had seen them before. Russian made deep water explosives. He didn't recognise any of the men, and was struggling to put it all together until the boat changed angle slightly and the sun glare moved off the wheelhouse window.

He recognised the man who was driving the boat, his face

twisted into a grimace. How he had located them was a question for another time, Andrews, however, knew well enough their intentions.

Tossing the binoculars onto the deck, he raced back into the wheelhouse and snatched up the radio. He had to make contact with them before it was too late. He had to let them know there was somebody down in the water.

CHAPTER TWENTY-EIGHT

Rainwater paced the floor, glancing at the screen every few seconds as he listened to the chatter from the open line to Andrews's boat. Communication had stopped, but he could hear well enough that something was wrong. He could clearly hear Andrews on the radio, although his words were frustratingly unclear, coming in snatches of half heard sentences. Ross kept his distance and watched as Rainwater paced, pausing only to take a swig out of the whisky bottle, which he was carrying loosely by his side. Knowing it was no use, Rainwater spoke again into the phone.

"Andrews? Andrews? What the hell's happening out there? Why haven't you got her out of the water yet?"

As expected, there was no response.

"Fuck!" Rainwater grunted, taking another huge drink, which further stoked the fire in his belly. Several things came to him at once, triggering a mixture of emotions from rage, to sorrow, to frustration. He realised he was completely helpless to do anything to help, and that by not going along with Andrews when given a chance, he had relegated himself to mere spectator. The more he thought about it, the more he hated himself. He should have suspected she would do something like this. Not the Clara of old of course. She would have known better, but the new, celebrity Clara, the fake one who was trying to live up to the portrayal the media had of her, most certainly would do something so stupid and reckless.

The thing that surprised him most was his lack of reaction when first seeing the creature. He had expected to be terrified, expecting the sight of it to dredge up memories from the last encounter. Instead, it was indifference. He had lived with the horror for so long that he had built up a kind of immunity. He didn't even blame the creature. It was just a product of nature, a slave to its instinctive nature. If there was any blame to be placed, he put it firmly at his feet. True enough, he felt anger towards Clara for putting herself in such a dangerous situation, and he also felt old feelings, feelings he thought were long dead. He wasn't sure if he could exactly call it love. He wasn't even sure what that was anymore, but it was an overwhelming desire to do anything to protect her and keep her from harm, even if such a thing would be unwelcomed by her. Once again, the complete and utter helplessness of his situation became apparent, which was sated as always with the golden alcohol.

II

Tom, Jim, and Fernando, waited at the stern with the Russev's as the boat closed on its target. Tom and Fernando locked eyes across the steel framed device, able to communicate their concerns without words in the way only siblings can. Jim seemed indifferent, and if not for the visual differences, could have been one of the Russev's, such was his lack of concern.

In the wheelhouse, Greg slowed, ignoring the radio calls from the other boat as he lined up alongside and pulled back on the throttle.

"Let it go!" he screamed over his shoulder.

The Russev's and Jim shoved with everything they had. Tom and Fernando did their best to make a show of it. Just as the device slipped over the side and plunged into the ocean, Andrews raced out on deck.

"You assholes!" he raged. "There's a diver down there!"

Andrews was staring at Tom as he said it. Greg hurried out of the wheelhouse just as the stern of the boat was thrown out of the water by the concussion wave, as the bomb exploded on contact with the cave roof seventy feet below.

III

Clara's first thought was that the creature had attacked. A deafening rumble surrounded her seconds before the roof of the cave collapsed, huge boulders crushing several of the creature's eggs as it buried the animal itself under tons of rubble. Only because she was safely tucked away in the crevasse was she saved from certain death. Dropping the camera, she braced her hands and feet against the confines of her space, waiting for the chaos to subside. She bit down on her regulator, vaguely aware that if the air tank were to slam against the wall of the cave too hard, it would explode, killing her instantly. Dust and silt were thrown up from the impact, making a claustrophobic blanket of darkness as her torch was obscured.

Oh God, please don't let me die here.

After what felt like an eternity, the noise subsided. Against the odds, she was still alive. She waited for the dirt thrown up from the floor of the cave to dissipate and the pace of her heart to slow, then surveyed the damage. A huge section of the roof had collapsed. Directly above her, through the twisted rock, she could see the distant pale blue of the surface waters. Her eye, however, was drawn back to the remaining roof above her, which looked ready to collapse in at any given second. She knew if that happened, she would die. There would be no rescue, no escape, and no second chance. Her heart pounded against her ribcage, and she forced herself to calm and stop sucking such large mouthfuls of air. She closed her eyes and looked within herself, looking for the Clara of old, the one she had buried someplace deep in order to keep up with the public perception of who she should be. She didn't need the current incarnation of herself anymore, the one who attended charity lunches and book signings, the one who flew first class to movie premieres and hobnobbed with other tanned celebrities. She needed the old Clara. The one who didn't mind getting her hands dirty, the one who was fearless and resourceful, the one who was selfless and able to think on her feet. The one who had led two grown men in scaling the Ross Ice Shelf some five years earlier on what was deemed to be a suicide mission.

Clara knew she was in there somewhere, buried deep and forgotten, cast aside in order to build a new life. She would know what to do, she would know how to react, and she would-

She froze. The rocks further down the cave began to move and were shoved aside as the creature rose from beneath. It flicked its tail and pushed its snout against the pulpy remains of the eggs that were crushed, then in a single motion, launched itself at the crevasse where Clara was still wedged. She bit down hard and tried to push back as the creature smashed snout first into the cave, as it tried to get to what it perceived as the attacker of it and its young.

CHAPTER TWENTY-NINE

Greg had been thrown off balance by the explosion and along with the others, had been knocked to the ground. He was vaguely aware of someone from the other boat shouting at him as he pulled himself back to his feet. The plans had been to slow, drop the bomb and accelerate away from the blast zone, however, something had gone wrong, and be it miscommunication or just poor timing, they had been caught in the resulting explosion. The rear of the Lady of the Water had been tossed towards Andrews' boat, and Greg was praying there wasn't any damage to Victor's vessel, which might cost him another body part or worse. He squinted at the man on the boat opposite, who was pacing and screaming. If he was a government official, he didn't look the part. He was wearing shorts and a white t-shirt, and his hair was sticking up in the back. Greg staggered closer to the stern to hear him.

"What the hell did you just do?" Andrews screamed, the prominent vein in his forehead pulsing in fury.

"What I had to," Greg replied with a grin. "That bastard fish of yours ruined my life."

"You fucking idiot! There's a diver down there in the water!"

Greg froze, the grin melting off his face. This wasn't what he wanted. Not more death. His issue was with the creature and the creature alone.

"I didn't know, how could I know? You should have warned us," Greg stammered.

"I tried but you didn't answer your damn radio."

Tom and the others had overheard, and now all of them stood on deck looking at Greg.

"We need to get down and help. Whoever is down there could be trapped," Joanne said.

"Not with that creature in the water. No way," Fernando said.

"Creature is dead. My bomb very powerful," Pavel interjected.

Andrews glanced inside the open wheelhouse door to the monitor, but the feed was dead.

"I don't have any diving gear on board this boat," Andrews

said. "Do you have anyone with diving experience that can get down there?"

"Jim, you've taken diving lessons haven't you?" Fernando asked.

"I'm not going down there. No way."

"Come on, we need you."

"Forget it. I'm not risking my own skin for someone I don't know."

"Is that what you said to Clayton?" Joanne said before she could stop herself.

"You should watch your mouth, bitch," Jim spat back.

"Hey, don't talk to her like that," Tom said, shoving Jim in the shoulder.

"Fuck her, and fuck you. You don't tell me what to do."

"Look, we don't have time for this. Someone needs to go down there and help them," Marie said.

"I'll go."

They looked around to see Greg struggling to climb into a wetsuit.

"You can't go, you're..." Fernando's words died in his throat.

"Disabled, I know. I'm also the only qualified diver here. Now, will you shut up and help me into this wetsuit?"

Tom hurried to Greg, helping him to fasten the suit.

"Thanks," Greg muttered. "Air tanks are in there," he said pointing to the small door by the wheelhouse. "Grab that box from in there too."

Tom did as he was told, grabbing the scuba tank as Fernando dragged out the box behind it.

"What happened to not caring?" Tom said as he helped Greg to strap on the heavy scuba tank.

"Whatever you lot might think of me, I'm not some heartless prick. As much as I hate this monster, I don't hate it enough to get more blood on my hands. Trust me, I've been there."

"Will you be okay down there, with your hand I mean?" Tom said.

Greg nodded. "Got it covered."

He walked over to the box which Fernando had dragged out on deck and removed the lid.

"What is it?" Tom asked as he looked inside.

"Pegasus thruster. Single diver propeller to aid underwater movement. These things can be pretty nippy. Can get up to quite a speed too. Clip it onto my scuba tank will ya?"

"How do you control it with just one hand?" Tom asked as he strapped the elongated black unit with the propeller at the rear onto Greg's scuba tank.

"It's pretty simple really," he said, grabbing the cable attached to the unit. At the end was a contoured hand controller with a grey button on top.

"I can pretty much do it all with my thumb. I press the button, the prop kicks in, and I get a speed boost."

"Fast?" Tom asked.

"I hope so. The bugger is pretty powerful, so it should get me down there sharpish to help this diver and get him back to the surface."

"Her," Andrews shouted.

"What's that?" Greg replied, looking over his shoulder.

"Her. The diver is a woman."

"You let a woman dive down there with that thing in the water?"

"Trust me, it's not like I had a choice. Now, can we hurry this along?"

Greg nodded and walked to the transom, as Pavel opened the hatch leading to the diving platform at the rear. As Greg went to pass, the Russian grabbed him by the upper arm, his grip vice like as he whispered in Greg's ear. "Don't die down there. Remember, you still owe Mr Mallone money."

"Thanks for the support, Pavel," Greg said, pulling his arm free. "I'll try my best."

Greg sat on the platform, his feet in the water. Adrenaline surged through him. He hadn't been in the ocean since he'd lost his hand, and almost his life, and it took every ounce of effort to keep the memories of what happened repressed. Tom brought out the facemask and helped Greg put it on.

"Alright," the Australian said, unable to keep the waver out of his voice, "keep an eye out for me. I'll go down there and take a look. When we get back, get us out of the water quick."

"Got it," Tom said.

Greg put the regulator in his mouth and took two deep breaths, then gave the thumbs up. He shuffled to the edge then stopped and removed the mouthpiece. "You have to believe I didn't want this to work out like this. I never wanted to hurt anyone." He replaced the mouthpiece and shuffled over the edge as the others watched, disappearing beneath the surface in a torrent of bubbles.

CHAPTER THIRTY

Bracing against the wall as best she could, Clara was powerless to do anything but watch as the creature lunged and snapped, as it tried to pull her from her sanctuary. She was remarkably calm as the giant dagger like teeth ground and clipped off the rock. Every time the creature opened its mouth, she could feel the change in temperature between the cool water and the heat of the monsters maw, and the suction as seawater was pulled into its depths, threatening to take her with it.

I'm going to die.

It was with calm that she readily accepted her fate. There seemed little point in fighting it. Already, the creature had broken away some of the rock, and she knew it wouldn't be long until it had made a large enough hole to pluck her out and devour her. She wondered if it would hurt, if she would be aware as those fifteen inch teeth punctured her body, if she would feel her bones crushed as she was swallowed into its stinking, black gullet.

II

Greg saw immediately the damage done by the explosive they had dropped. The cave roof had been obliterated, the original entrance completely sealed by debris. Inside, directly below, Greg could see the creature as it lunged and snapped at the wall. Between each thrust, he could see the pale blue wetsuit of the trapped diver.

A mixture of feelings surged through him. Guilt. Excitement. Fear. None able to quite take control, and content instead, to swirl around his brain and wait for him to make a decision. He hadn't considered what he was actually going to do when he arrived before he had made the dive. It had seemed like the most natural and right thing to do under the circumstances. The half idea he had formulated, seemed like nothing but a suicide mission now that the creature was within sight. He took a moment to look at it, hating how despite himself, he had a certain respect for its sheer power and majesty. It took another lunge by the creature at the diver trapped to spur him into action. He swam closer to the hole, his thumb hovering over the trigger for the Pegasus thruster. He didn't even really know if it would be fast enough to keep him at a safe distance from the creature, and yet, he found that very fact to fill him with euphoria. As he approached, and could better see the powerful tentacles and the immense flipper-tail of the creature, he was transported back to the day in the cage. The day he had been so overwhelmingly stunned to see such an incredible creature, which against all odds, had remained hidden from mankind for so long. Anger replaced wonder, and he knew it was time to do what he came to do before he lost his nerve. Taking a second to compose himself, Greg depressed the button held in his remaining hand, activating the twin propellers attached to his air tanks and launching him towards the hole where the cave roof once stood.

The reaction of the creature was immediate. Still infuriated by the attack on its lair, it turned towards Greg and snapped its jaws, the concussion wave enough to rock the Australian as he circled away.

The creature didn't give chase, instead, it turned back towards Clara, smashing its nose into the tiny gap in the cave wall as it tried to pluck her free.

Greg came again, this time arcing towards the creature from the front, skimming down past its head and massive eye.

I'm close enough to reach out and touch it.

He said to himself as he dove under its giant flipper and circled around again.

At least I could if I had a hand.

A mad cackle of laughter reverberated around his skull, as he came again at the creature, aiming for its eye then veering away at the last second. Once again, the creature snapped.

Greg circled away, marvelling at the manoeuvrability he was afforded by the thruster. His excitement lasted only seconds, however. As this time, the creature didn't return its attention to Clara.

It was coming for him.

He sped through the opening in the roof, sensing more than seeing the creature smashing through in pursuit. He pushed his flippered feet together, as he tried to eke every last drop of speed from the Pegasus thruster. He glanced over his shoulder and had to swallow the scream which lurched up into his throat. His entire field of vision was taken up by the creature. Suddenly, the ocean didn't quite seem like such a wide and expansive place. He considered going deeper, back into one of the other caves, which were scattered across the floor of the ocean. Instead, he ascended, hoping the diver he was desperately trying to free had taken the opportunity to get to the surface.

III

Clara didn't think she would be able to move. She watched the creature go, a streak of green and grey as it lurched through the hole in the roof in pursuit of whatever had grabbed its attention. After the utter chaos and violence of its repeated attacks as it tried to get to her, the silence in which she now lay was somehow worse. She could feel her body trembling, her breath ragged as she gulped in air, grateful just to be breathing. She wasn't sure what it was that set her into motion. Partly, it was the thought of the creature coming back to finish what it started. Partly, it was the fear of the roof finally giving way and trapping her forever, leaving her destined to die a slow, painful death, as she waited for her air to run out. Mostly, though, it was the thought that life would go on without her. She felt an intense need, a desire to live it, to take part in the world as one of its citizens, not to die in a cave and possibly never to be recovered. She couldn't bear the idea of her parents having to bury an empty coffin. That image spurred her to move. She pulled herself free, glancing at the huge gouges in the rock, and kicked furiously, making for the bobbing shadow of the boats hull, curious to see the second boat alongside it and wondering where it had come from.

IV

It was a life and death situation. Greg was in no doubt of that. He no longer dared look over his shoulder, and didn't have to. He could feel the sheer mass of the creature behind him. Using the weight of his body to change direction, he was becoming aware that

RETURN TO THE DEEP

he was nowhere near as efficiently designed for underwater manoeuvrability than his pursuer. Despite his best effort, the snapping behemoth was closing on him. He absently wondered if he had given the diver enough time to escape, a thought followed quickly by the idea that for all he knew, it could be a waste of time, and said diver could already be dead, pierced by one of the creature's giant teeth. Either way, he had done all he could, and had given them all the time he could spare to escape. As powerful as it was, the Pegasus thruster had a limited fuel supply, and he couldn't even begin to think about the repercussions if it expired before he had managed to get to safety. He angled to his left, catching a glimpse of his giant pursuer in his peripheral vision as he changed direction. Larger and slower to turn, Greg bought himself some precious distance as the creature turned to follow. In the distance, he could see the diver making for the surface, nothing but a dark blue shadow against the paler backdrop of the expansive ocean. His distraction almost cost him, and he instinctively veered to the right, ascending at the same time as the creature closed, biting down on the area of ocean he had occupied just seconds earlier. Trying to squeeze every last ounce of performance from the Pegasus, Greg focussed on reaching the boats without trying to think about how he might find the time to board it before he was devoured. He smiled inside, and wondered if he had lost his mind.

V

On the surface, there was little evidence of the life and death struggles going on beneath the surface. Andrews had seen Clara free herself from the cave wall, from the camera, which she had left behind, and was now readying the tranquilizer harpoon. Loaded with a powerful drug used to stun Bull elephants in the wild, Andrews knew he would likely only have one shot. The dart acted quickly, however, was likely to infuriate the creature until the drug took effect. He was just finishing attaching the dart when Clara broke the surface of the water. He hurried to the stern, holding out a hand as she swam towards him. Rather than watch her, he was staring beyond into the ocean, expecting to see the mammoth head appear beneath her and snatch her back into the abyss when she was so close to freedom. However, that didn't happen, and she grasped Andrews's hand as he pulled her from the water, gritting his teeth as she scrambled onto the deck. She pulled off her goggles, spat out her regulator, and unclipped her tanks, letting them fall to the deck. She took a second to appreciate it, the feel of the baking sun warming her skin, the feeling of fresh air going into her lungs, even the sight of her shadow, narrow as it stretched across the deck. She knew she had been lucky to survive.

"Jesus, Clara," Andrews said as he turned back to the harpoon gun, "you could have been killed down there. What the hell were you thinking?"

"There's no time for that now. That thing is on the loose."

"I know, I was watching the feed," Andrews snapped.

"Did you see the eggs?"

"Yeah, I saw them," Andrews said, his throat suddenly dry. He swallowed, coughed, and then turned back to the weapon. "I called it in. The fleet are on their way."

"How long?"

"Too long. I'm gonna have to tranq it."

"You can't do that without killing it, can you?" She asked, pushing the wet hair from her forehead.

"At this point, I don't care. I just want this stopped."

Clara nodded. Even as a child, she had always been pro animal conservation, always believed that there was no viable reason to kill any other living creature, and had even fought against the harming of the creature during the first encounter. Something came to her then, an epiphany of sorts. Something which she must have always known on some level, but had never acknowledged.

"This is all my fault," she said to Andrews.

"What do you mean?"

"Everything that's happening here and now, it's all my fault."

"How exactly do you figure that?" Andrews said as he snapped the barrel of the harpoon rifle into position.

"In the ice cave. You weren't there of course, but I was. Rainwater and me...Mackay..." she lowered her head and continued to speak, unable to look at him. "We put this thing back into the water. We allowed it to swim free. If we'd have just left it there on the bank, it would have died."

"And Russo would have lived, which means there was a good chance you wouldn't have."

"That's not the point. Russo was wounded, we could have handled it."

"Clara, please, I-"

He was stopped mid-sentence by the commotion from the other boat. Andrews looked at them, the teens, as they shouted and pointed. Andrews and Clara turned, squinting at the sun as it scattered gold across the surface of the water. They still saw it though, and Andrews felt the unforgettable numb ache of terror creep up on him like an old friend. For the first time, he appreciated how completely out of his depth he was. Although he had seen the creature up close countless times in the facility in Florida, he was always safe. Always on the surface or in the underground viewing area. Now however, things had changed. Now he was in a tiny boat on the ocean, and the enormous wake that rolled towards them was showing no sign of slowing.

"Jesus Christ," he muttered as he picked up the rifle.

"You're shaking," Clara said, glancing from the wake to Andrews.

"I'll be fine."

"Bullshit you will. Give it to me. I'll take the shot."

"I can't do that; I have a responsibility to-"

"Damn it, Andrews, just hand me the weapon."

Andrews did as he was told, partially glad to be free of the responsibility. Clara took the gun and walked to the stern, then climbed up on the transom. She spread her feet, distributing her weight, then tucked the rifle into her shoulder, nestling it there and getting comfortable as she watched the wake roll closer. For the first time, she truly understood how Rainwater must have felt that first night back on the fishing boat, when he had seen a wake much bigger than this one approach and broadside his father's fishing boat. She could see the psychological damage that could cause, and felt bad for giving him such a hard time about it. Pushing it aside, she concentrated on her breathing, on matching her movements with the steady bob and sway of the boat. Less easy to push aside was the duality of the situation, the similarity to another time when she was in an almost identical position. Back then of course, she had been bullied into it by Russo, who was refusing to rescue Rainwater and his crew from their boat, which was under attack from the creature unless she took the shot for him. Like all the memories of that time, it came back to her with an oozing ease, the memories, ones she knew she would never be able to forget.

Murmurs from those on deck pulled Russo's attention back to the water, just in time to see the creature smash broadside into the boat a second time, making deck boards explode as it was spun around, the resulting wake slewing the Victorious aside and furthering the distance between it and the Lisa Marie. Already wounded, the fishing boat began to slide slowly into the ocean, its bow lifting out of the water as its stern sank. The crew scrambled to stay above the waterline as the creature retreated again, pausing to snag Ox's body where it bobbed on the surface, swallowing it in a singular bite, as it once again raced away and readied a new attack.

"If you don't help them, they'll die," Clara said, and Russo turned to her. All eyes were on him, and he grinned.

"Not until I get my shot."

"They're innocent people!" She screamed.

"Innocent? Those people interfered in a government operation. They don't deserve my help."

"That's not for you to decide, they need to be tried in a court."

Russo's grin faltered for a second, then he shrugged.

"Either way, nobody steps foot on this boat until I get my shot."

"Then do it, take the damn shot and help them!" she said again, watching as the creature prepared to attack.

"I can't risk missing. If they hadn't interfered, none of this would have happened. They only have themselves to blame."

"Give me the harpoon," Clara said.

"What do you mean?"

"You say you will help them if you make this shot, and then give it to me. I'll make sure it hits the target. You get those people out of the water."

"You better not be lying to me."

"Hurry up and hand me the damn harpoon," she said, glaring at Russo.

He did as she asked, and was about to instruct her on how to operate it when she deftly swung it onto her shoulder, adjusted her aim, and readied to fire.

"You've done this before," Russo said, genuinely impressed.

"Don't talk to me. Just get those people out of the water before I change my mind."

Russo turned to Mito and nodded, and the officer ran to the lifeboat station. Clara aimed at the water, allowing her breathing to calm, making sure her feet were spread evenly as she watched the beast circle.

"No games," Russo hissed over her shoulder, the smell of his minty breath close to her face. "If you miss or try to screw me, I won't be responsible for what happens."

She could feel the eyes of everyone on deck boring into her and tried her best to ignore it. The sun was hot on her neck and a trickle of sweat ran down the inside of her nose. She adjusted her aim slightly, paused, and spoke to Russo.

"I'm, ready. You'd better stick to your word."

"That all depends on you,"

She ignored him, readying herself as the creature charged, looking to finish off the stricken boat, which was rapidly losing its fight to stay afloat.

She relaxed her shoulders and exhaled as the grey streak raced along below the surface. Sunlight glittered off the water, making it difficult to be sure where she was aiming. She squeezed the trigger, hoping against hope to land a fleshy spot on the creature; somewhere the barbed harpoon could find purchase. She had expected a deafening roar of gunfire when she squeezed the trigger, but instead, the weapon fired with a hollow pneumatic Whumph, as the harpoon speared into the water, burying itself in the soft flesh above the creature's eye. The harpoon sheared through tangled clusters of nerves, igniting pain receptors, which sent the charging beast into agonising spasms. Rearing away from the crippled Lisa Marie, the creature dived deep, trying to cool the searing pain of the dart in its flesh. Clara lowered the spent harpoon, then turned to watch Mito as he loaded its survivors into the lifeboat and winched it to the deck. Clara dropped the harpoon, trying to ignore Russo's oozing smile.

Snapping back to the present, she focussed her attention on the wake. Without moving, she spoke to Andrews, the calm tone of her voice masking the terror that surged through her. "Swimmer in the water," she said as she peered through the sight. "Get ready to pull him out."

She didn't look - her attention was fully on the wake now, but she felt Andrews move, and could sense him beside her, leaning over the rear of the boat and waiting.

"For God's sake, don't miss," Andrews said.

Clara didn't answer. She simply watched and waited for the creature to be close enough to hit.

VI

The Pegasus thruster was almost out of fuel. The monotonous whine had started to falter, the tone slowly but surely decreasing in pitch, and with it, speed. He had already acknowledged that he was likely about to die, yet, was too stubborn to accept it. With nothing to lose, he moved closer to the surface, skimming just a couple of feet beneath the waves. The Pegasus spluttered again, further killing his speed. Just twenty feet behind him, the creature followed, determined in its rage not to abandon its prey. Greg could see the hull of the two boats ahead of him. They were tantalisingly close, and he was filled with a renewed energy. He angled towards the nearest hull, hoping the creature would abandon its pursuit if it sensed the twin hulls in the water. The stern of the nearest boat was to his left now, and he could see the warped shape of an arm reaching out for him on the surface. He cursed his disability. In order to grab the waiting hand, he would have to drop the control for the Pegasus thruster. An ordinary man would have simply been able to switch the control to the opposite hand. However, for him of course, that wasn't an option. Greg knew he would have to be reliant on another miracle, another against all odds, a one in a million gamble. It would need perfect timing, and there would be only one chance to get it right. He would have to release his grip on the control, grab the hand, and then hope its owner would act quickly enough to pull him to safety. He didn't like to think about the hundreds of things that could go wrong. A missed grab, a slight timing error, a loss of grip would be all it would take almost to guarantee his death. He turned on his side, arm outstretched above the surface. His head broke the water and he could see the government agent as he leaned over the edge, face set in a determined frown.

Come on, Greg, make this count.

He dropped the control at the last possible second, the power to the twin propellers of the Pegasus instantly dying. His arm made solid contact, and he felt fingers digging into his forearm as he locked his grip on Andrews's arm, and yet, it only lasted a split second. His momentum dragged him past the stern. As quickly as it had arrived, the grip of his saviour was gone.

Panic.

All at once, he was incredibly aware of everything around him. He rolled onto his back, seeing the giant tsunami like wave as it came at him, just seconds away from smashing into him. He couldn't see the creature itself, the sun was too bright on the surface. He closed his eyes, waiting for the inevitable, hoping it would be quick.

Below the surface, the creature opened its jaws, knowing its prey was incapacitated. It was about to devour it when the dart hit home, Clara having hit the same place as the first time around, landing the dart just above the creatures milky eye. At precisely the same time, Andrews grabbed Greg at the second time of asking, grabbing a twin handful of the shoulders of his wetsuit and yanking him into the boat, where both tumbled to the deck.

The creature whirled away from the point of impact. The wake rolling past both boats and making Clara lose her footing. She dropped the harpoon, pin wheeling her arms as the boat rocked beneath her. She rocked forward, her head dipping towards the ocean. She was going in. She couldn't avoid it. Just as she lost her fight with gravity, she felt strong arms around her waist as she was pulled onto the safety of the deck by Andrews, where she joined him on the deck beside Greg, the three of them breathing heavily.

"Thanks," she panted as she got up.

The three of them could hear shouting from the other boat, and looked up just in time to see the wake. Infuriated by the attack, the creature slammed into the hull of the boat, launching the stern out of the ocean. Like ragdolls, Clara, Greg, and Andrews, were tossed into the ocean.

CHAPTER THIRTY-ONE

"Please, you have to do something," Tom said to Pavel. They surrounded him now, yet the Russian seemed unfazed. Instead, he and his brother watched proceedings unfold with indifference.

"You have to help," Joanne added.

"We don't get paid to help. Just to make sure boat comes back in one piece," Pavel replied, his tone as uninterested and flat as always.

"But they need us. We can't just watch them die."

Pavel shrugged. "Not our problem."

"You assholes," Joanne hissed.

Alexi mumbled something in Russian to his brother, who replied in his own language. Both laughed and looked at Joanne with matching predatory smiles.

"I can drive a boat," Marie said. "I mean, my father has a speedboat, but I could get us close enough to help."

"Alright," Tom said, glaring at the Russevs, "let's do it."

"No," Pavel said, taking a half step towards Marie. "This is Mr Mallone's boat. Nobody drive."

"But they need our help," Joanne screamed.

"Not our problem."

"We're not afraid of you," Joanne said, her eyes proving her a liar. "You can't stop us."

Pavel simply smiled, daring her to test him.

"Forget them," Tom said. "Go ahead, Marie."

"Are you crazy?" Jim said, stepping between Marie and the wheelhouse door. "We can't do anything to help. Do you want to attract that thing over to us and kill us too?"

"Get out of the way, Jim," Joanne said, holding his gaze.

"No."

"I'll tell them, I swear I will."

"Tell us what?" Tom said, looking from Joanne to Jim.

"I'll save you the trouble," Jim said with an arrogant smile. "Your girlfriend has it into her head that I had something to do with Clayton dying."

"You did it. You told me!" Joanne screamed.

"Did I?" Jim said with a smile. "Do you have any proof of that?"

"I know you did it. You near enough told me."

"You crazy bitch, you really have issues," Jim said.

"Hey, I already told you, you don't talk to her like that," Tom said, and then was interrupted by Fernando before he could say anymore.

"What's your problem, man?" Fernando said.

"Nothing, I'm just trying to get the rest of you to see sense."

Something snapped in Joanne then. The built up frustration mingled with fear made her react. She lunged at Jim with the fork she had taken earlier in one hand. "I'll kill you, you liar!" She raged.

Marie shied away as Tom and Fernando restrained her, trying to wrestle the knife free. Jim just grinned at her. A secret grin, a grin that told her she was right, even if nobody would believe her.

Tom and Fernando managed to calm her, Tom dragging her away from Jim to the rear of the boat.

"That guy needs to control that bitch of his," Jim said with a grin just seconds before Fernando punched him, a huge looping right hand that caught him flush on the jaw. Jim staggered backwards into the wheelhouse as Fernando stalked forward, looking to finish the job.

"Stop!" Pavel snapped.

Everyone froze and looked at him, trying to decipher what was going on behind those cold dead eyes.

"Look," he said, nodding towards the other boat.

II

Clara, Andrews and Greg were huddled in the water, waiting for their inevitable death. The creature approached them, and yet, didn't attack. Instead, it moved past them and approached the hull of their boat, which was sitting low in the water. The creature nudged the hull, pushing it away from its stranded crew.

"What the hell is it doing?" Andrews whispered as they treaded water.

"It's toying with us," Clara replied, feeling so sick with fear it almost presented itself as a giggle. "I've seen this kind of behaviour by killer whales when they're hunting sea lions."

"This isn't normal. The adult never behaved this way."

"This is a juvenile. It's playing with its food," she replied, locking eyes with Andrews.

"It's okay, the dart should take effect soon."

"We're gonna die, aren't we?" Greg said, his face gaunt and haunted.

"Not necessarily," Clara replied. "There's a chance it might-"

The creature exploded out of the water, its massive jaws crushing down on Clara's body as it rose out of the water. Andrews heard screaming, everything seeming to happen in slow motion. The creature reached the height of its momentum, and for a split second, paused in mid-air. Andrews locked eyes with Clara, her upper body and one mangled, twisted leg still hanging from the creature's mouth. Her face was turned towards him, blood pouring from her nostrils and mouth.

Good God, she's aware.

Andrews thought as the creature sank back beneath the waves, taking its prize with it. Only then did Andrews realise the screams were coming from him. It acted as a trigger point. Both Greg and Andrews started to swim, legs kicking furiously, heads down as they made for their respective boats. Andrews swam through the bloody surface waters, taking huge gulps of air as he waited for his turn, and for the demon in the water to take its next prize. Sensing the motion on the surface, the creature swallowed the mangled remains of Clara and gave chase. As the signal from its prey split into two, the creature changed direction, swimming after Greg.

Andrews reached the hull of the boat, hauling himself up and out of the water, and onto the deck, turning to watch the wake cut through the water.

Once again, Greg was sure he was about to die. His luck was out. The creature had chosen him as its next victim, and the thought of suffering the same fate as the woman filled him with a horror even greater than when he was forced to cut off his hand. He could see his boat, the white hull too far away. He knew he would never reach it in time. He could hear the kids he had brought out to sea with the intention of helping him, screaming at him to swim faster, to hurry, yet inside, he knew it was over. He was beaten. He stopped and turned to face his fate, wanting to meet it head on, and not be taken by surprise like the woman had been. He watched the wake as it streaked towards him, and could see the creature below the surface, an immense torpedo as it streaked through the water towards him. Greg closed his eyes, praying it wouldn't hurt.

The explosion was deafening.

Greg gasped, throwing an arm up to protect his face as the water erupted in an explosion of blood and bone. Confused, he watched as the creature drifted past him, the entire upper portion of it skull missing and spewing gallon upon gallon of blood into the ocean. Greg turned to face the Lady of the Water, peering up at the faces who watched from the sun-baked deck. Pavel Russev lowered the smoking rocket launcher and dropped it to the deck as Tom threw a life ring towards the exhausted Australian, however, he didn't reach for it. He had to know, he had to be sure. Taking a deep breath, he ducked his head beneath the waves and watched as the creature sank head first towards the bottom, leaving a bloody cloud of bone and flesh behind it. He had expected the death of the creature to fill him with some kind of joy or relief, however, he found if anything, he felt worse. His selfishness had cost more lives, and he knew they would only add to the burden he had already been forced to live with. As he was pulled out of the water by the Russev's, he began to weep.

CHAPTER THIRTY-TWO

The Navy ships that Andrews had called in duly arrived on site as the sun began to dip beneath the horizon line. More than a dozen vessels now surrounded the two boats, which hadn't moved since the attack. Andrews stood on the deck of the two hundred and twenty foot vessel sent by Tomlinson, a heavy blanket draped over his shoulders. He watched as everyone from Greg's boat was handcuffed and transported to a police boat that was on scene. They had already checked the paperwork for the boat and linked it back to a known arms dealer in New York. He stood and watched as the vessel was searched under the glow of spotlights from the surrounding boats.

"Sir."

Andrews turned to greet the man in military fatigues that approached.

"What is it?"

"We found the remains of the creature, sir."

Andrews nodded, not quite sure how he felt about it yet.

"What about the cave?"

"We found and destroyed the eggs as ordered, however, we discovered something unexpected."

"What did you find?"

"Deeper into the cave, there were five egg casings that had already hatched."

Andrews felt his stomach plunge into his shoes.

"Are you absolutely sure?"

"Positive, sir. We've taken samples to the lab for analysis."

Andrews barely heard him, instead, he stared out over the ocean, trying to put his thoughts into some kind of order. There was a giddy lightness, some heightened feeling of dread, which left a sour taste at the back of his throat.

Five eggs.

Five of these beasts free and on the loose.

"Sir?" the man said, plainly confused at Andrews's vacancy.

"Sorry, say again?"

"I said Commander Tomlinson wants you to make contact with him right away."

Andrews nodded. "I will, I just need to make a quick phone call."

"He was insistent, sir. He said it's important."

"So is this," Andrews muttered. "I have to tell someone I couldn't keep the promise I made."

The man in the fatigues hesitated for a moment, and then headed back towards the busy command centre of the vessel.

CHAPTER THIRTY-THREE

Rainwater was packing his bag when Ross walked into the cabin. The burly Scotsman folded his arms, watching Rainwater pack.

"Goin' somewhere?" he said.

"I have to go back. I can't stay here."

"I thought you'd come ere tae get away from yer old life," the Scot said.

Rainwater stopped packing and turned to face Ross, his eyes pink and puffy. "I can't just stay here and accept what happened."

"It's only been a few days, laddie. Terrible, terrible news about this lassie. I'll grant ye that. But ye can't do anythin' by goin back there. It won't bring her back."

Rainwater opened his mouth, almost telling Ross what Andrews had told him about the other creatures, which were somewhere in the ocean. Rainwater was still haunted by the way that Andrews had sounded when he called, how flat and empty his voice when he said the words Rainwater would have done anything not to have to hear.

She's gone, Henry. I'm so sorry. I couldn't save her.

"There's something I have to do. I need to face this head on. I can't explain. Something's changed."

"Aye, I see that. Ye haven' touched a drop 'o' the booze since ye were told about that lassie passin' on."

"I don't need it anymore," Rainwater said as he turned back towards his bag. "I used it to hide from this, but I know now I can't. I know what I'm supposed to do now."

"Ye know what mah brother would ah said te ye don' ye?"

"I can guess," Rainwater replied, almost managing a smile. "But he'd also understand why I'm going back."

"Aye, he would," Ross said. "That's why ahm comin wi ye."

Rainwater stopped and glanced at Ross. "I can't ask you to do that."

"Ah didn't say ye did. This is mah call."

"If you're anything like your brother, I guess talking you out of it isn't an option."

"Ye got that right. We Mackay's are a stubborn family. Whatever ye have to deal with, I'll help ye. I'll also help ye make sure ye stay away from the drink. That's a dark road, lad, one ye already walked on."

"Thanks, I really do appreciate it. If you're coming with me though, you should know exactly what I'm going back to do."

"Then ye better start talkin', lad."

II

An hour later, Rainwater was sitting in the passenger seat of Ross's mud splattered black jeep, watching the Scot lock up the cabin. He had told him all about the creatures that were on the loose, and that, one way or the other, he was going back to finish what had started all those years ago. Ross jogged to the car and climbed into the driver's side, rubbing his hands together against the cold.

"Right, let's get to the airport and get this show on the road," he said as he shifted into gear and pulled away from the cabin, leaving the peace and solitude behind. Rainwater didn't answer. He stared out of the window, waging a war with his own internal demons, who even now were trying to tempt him back off the wagon. He tried to close his eyes and immediately saw Clara's screaming face.

No.

He thought sleep was something that would evade him for some time yet. Instead, he contented himself with staring at the lush Scottish hills, the hues of green and brown a far cry away from where he knew his future lay, which was on the ocean. Shuffling down in his seat, he prepared himself for the journey ahead of what he knew he must do, no matter the cost.

EPILOGUE

The immense laboratory stretched for almost a quarter of a mile, its pristine white walls surrounding a space filled with the very latest in cutting edge genetics sequencing equipment. Its four hundred strong staff worked in unison, the very best in their field. Decker walked through the room, arms behind his back, one hand clasping the wrist of the other. He was greeted by a white haired, grinning scientist in a white coat and with a five day beard growth.

"It's done, Mr Decker," the scientist said, unable to hold off his grin.

"Walk with me," Decker said, not slowing. "You managed to stabilise the sequence?"

"Yes sir."

"So we can proceed with the cloning?"

"Yes sir."

Decker nodded. "What level of projected success rate?"

"Well sir, as you know, we were initially looking at around the seventy five percent range, however, due to the high quality of the samples you provided, I-"

"What level, Doctor Morris?"

"Ninety seven point five."

Decker nodded. "Excellent work. I'll see to it that you and your staff receive a healthy bonus."

"Thank you, Mr Decker. If I might ask though, now that you have the ability to create these creatures, what will you do with them?"

Decker smiled and came to a halt, looking down into the immense shallow pool below.

"Whatever I want to, Doctor Morris. Whatever I want to."

The doctor nodded as Decker looked into the pool. Inside, at various stages of artificial growth, were over a hundred eggs, some almost fully grown.

"It all just depends who's prepared to pay the best price," Decker muttered under his breath as he watched the work go on.

CHECK OUT OTHER GREAT DEEP SEA THRILLERS

MEGA
by Jake Bible

There is something in the deep. Something large. Something hungry. Something prehistoric.
And Team Grendel must find it, fight it, and kill it.
Kinsey Thorne, the first female US Navy SEAL candidate has hit rock bottom. Having washed out of the Navy, she turned to every drink and drug she could get her hands on. Until her father and cousins, all ex-Navy SEALS themselves, offer her a way back into the life: as part of a private, elite combat Team being put together to find and hunt down an impossible monster in the Indian Ocean. Kinsey has a second chance, but can she live through it?

THE BLACK
by Paul E Cooley

Under 30,000 feet of water, the exploration rig Leaguer has discovered an oil field larger than Saudi Arabia, with oil so sweet and pure, nations would go to war for the rights to it. But as the team starts drilling exploration well after exploration well in their race to claim the sweet crude, a deep rumbling beneath the ocean floor shakes them all to their core. Something has been living in the oil and it's about to give birth to the greatest threat humanity has ever seen.

"The Black" is a techno/horror-thriller that puts the horror and action of movies such as Leviathan and The Thing right into readers' hands. Ocean exploration will never be the same."

SEVEREDPRESS

twitter.com/severedpress

CHECK OUT OTHER GREAT
DEEP SEA THRILLERS

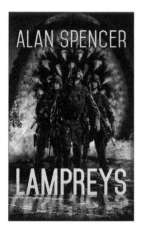

LAMPREYS
by Alan Spencer

A secret government tactical team is sent to perform a clean sweep of a private research installation. Horrible atrocities lurk within the abandoned corridors. Mutated sea creatures with insane killing abilities are waiting to suck the blood and meat from their prey.

Unemployed college professor Conrad Garfield is forced to assist and is soon separated from the team. Alone and afraid, Conrad must use his wits to battle mutated lampreys, infected scientists and go head-to-head with the biggest monstrosity of all.

Can Conrad survive, or will the deadly monsters suck the very life from his body?

DEEP DEVOTION
by M.C. Norris

Rising from the depths, a mind-bending monster unleashes a wave of terror across the American heartland. Kate Browning, a Kansas City EMT confronts her paralyzing fear of water when she traces the source of a deadly parasitic affliction to the Gulf of Mexico. Cooperating with a marine biologist, she travels to Florida in an effort to save the life of one very special patient, but the source of the epidemic happens to be the nest of a terrifying monster, one that last rose from the depths to annihilate the lost continent of Atlantis.

Leviathan, destroyer, devoted lifemate and parent, the abomination is not going to take the extermination of its brood well.

CHECK OUT OTHER GREAT
DEEP SEA THRILLERS

PREDATOR X
by C.J Waller

When deep level oil fracking uncovers a vast subterranean sea, a crack team of cavers and scientists are sent down to investigate. Upon their arrival, they disappear without a trace. A second team, including sedimentologist Dr Megan Stoker, are ordered to seek out Alpha Team and report back their findings. But Alpha team are nowhere to be found – instead, they are faced with something unexpected in the depths. Something ancient. Something huge. Something dangerous. Predator X

DEAD BAIT
by Tim Curran

A husband hell-bent on revenge hunts a Wereshark...A Russian mail order bride with a fishy secret...Crabs with a collective consciousness...A vampire who transforms into a Candiru...Zombie piranha...Bait that will have you crawling out of your skin and more. Drawing on horror, humor with a helping of dark fantasy and a touch of deviance, these 19 contemporary stories pay homage to the monsters that lurk in the murky waters of our imaginations. If you thought it was safe to go back in the water...Think Again!

Printed in Great Britain
by Amazon